# Sweet Summer Surprise

## A Steamy Age Gap Beach Town Romance

# Sadira Stone

Sadira Stone

# Sweet Summer Surprise

♥

***She came to the beach to find herself—and found him.***

When Danielle's cheating ex lures their kids away for a vacation-palooza with his new squeeze, he leaves her with a non-refundable beach rental in Trappers Cove. Glum and lonely, she settles in to lick her wounds—and some sinfully delicious gelato.

Enter Matteo, the ice-cream vendor's hunky nephew. Mamma mia! The gorgeous younger man is charming, seductive, and utterly undeterred by their age difference. Maybe a no-strings fling is just what she needs.

What starts as a steamy summer escape soon flares into something neither of them expected. Their chemistry sparks hotter than the Fourth of July, and for the first time in forever, Danielle feels truly seen and cherished.

But a divorced mom with real-life responsibilities can't afford to live in fantasyland, and Matteo's future is in this perfect beach town. The clock is ticking. Matteo has two weeks to convince her their summer love is the start of a happily ever after.

*Sweet Summer Surprise* was previously published as *Gelato Surprise.*

To Duncan, my HEA

**A note to readers:**
I do not use generative artificial intelligence in any part of my writing process. All my books were written by me, with feedback from my human editor and human beta readers. Different "authors" may make different choices, but I believe the best art comes from human minds, spirits, and hearts. Take that, robot overlords!

# Contents

# Chapter One

♥

"He did what?"

"Disneyland?"

"That bastard!"

Danielle Peters took a bracing gulp of cheap Chardonnay before facing six goggling eyes. She could always count on her book club posse to denounce her ex-husband's latest douchebaggery.

She heaved a sigh and slumped back on the sofa. "How can I say no? The kids really want to go, and it's the only time he can take them."

Cari clucked her tongue while topping off Danielle's glass. "Really? He just happens to get VIP tickets during the beach vacation you've taken with your kids every summer of their frickin' lives?"

"Typical divorced dad," Marie added with a snort. "Spoil the kids two weeks a year, then turn them over to Mom for all the hard stuff—school, lessons, sports, doctor's appointments..."

Danielle massaged her aching temples. "The new girlfriend arranged it. Some kind of work junket in Southern California. She's taking her sons too." Another detail to sour the pot: Jason had been seeing this woman only two months, and already he was folding their kids into her family. Considering his dating history, which, it turns out, overlapped their marriage by several years, this girlfriend would mostly likely be around just long enough for Olivia and Noah to get attached.

Since giving Jason the boot, she'd labored to keep the kids' lives as normal as possible, including their beloved summer kickoff, two weeks on the Washington shore. But how could she deny them this vacation-palooza: four amusement parks and a week in San Diego? If she said no, the kids would hate her for it.

"And he waits to tell you until it's too late to get a refund on your rental?" Marie shooed her cat off the coffee table and slid the tray of snacks toward Danielle. "I call bullshit. Now eat something before you pass out. You're too pale."

Danielle speared a cheese cube. "Looks like I won't be getting much sun this summer. Not at the beach, anyway." She popped the cheese into her mouth, but she might as well be chewing cardboard. Had her ex robbed her of that too? First their much-anticipated family beach trip, and now her love of food? Jason had a talent for sucking all the joy out of her life. Like a black hole.

"Why the hell not?" Laurie thumped the coffee table, interrupting Danielle's daydream of ejecting Jason from an airlock into the endless void of outer space.

She blinked at her friend. "Why not what?"

Cari pushed her glasses down her nose and fixed Danielle with a laser-sharp gaze. "You should totally do it."

"Do what?"

Marie's brisk nod made her chandelier earrings tinkle. "You're stuck with the rental. Why not use it? Beats hanging around Tacoma all by yourself. Especially on the Fourth of July."

An odd sensation slithered down Danielle's spine. Shiver of warning, or tingle of delight? "I haven't traveled alone since—well—ever."

"So?" Cari refilled Danielle's glass. "You've been renting that same beach house so long, it's like a second home. Only better because it's close to the beach."

"And lots of cute guys," Laurie added with a nudge.

Danielle snorted. "A cute guy is the last thing I need."

Marie pinged a kernel of popcorn off Danielle's forehead. "It's the first thing you need. Classic scenario, just like in that movie. Oh, what's it called?" She circled her wrist, conjuring the memory. "Divorced woman takes a vacation by herself, goes to..."

"Tuscany?" Laurie suggested.

"Wasn't it Greece?" Cari asked.

Danielle slouched further into the sofa. "I thought it was the Caribbean."

Marie huffed. "The point is, you need time alone to get your head on straight. Pretty hard to do when your kids are around, right?"

Her friend wasn't wrong. Though she loved her kids more than anyone or anything, they didn't leave her much time for quiet contemplation.

"And God knows you deserve some pampering. So take advantage of this mess and make silver-lining lemonade." Marie flashed a satisfied smile and slurped her wine.

Cari raised a finger. "Umm, I think you mean—"

Marie bounced another popcorn kernel off Cari's forehead. "When Walter left me, I felt like crawling under a rock. But I forced myself to book a spa weekend at Salish Lodge. Just me, myself, and a big pile of murder books. They treated me like a queen. I wasted zero time thinking about my ex." She thumped her chest. "I came back rested, relaxed, and ready to tackle my new life as a single mom."

Laurie nodded. "Isn't there a spa out by Trappers Cove? Sea Queen something?"

Danielle shrugged. Her previous visits to that kitschy Washington beach town centered around seashell hunting, go-karts, mini-golf, sampling saltwater taffy—family stuff. Other than a raucous brew pub and a handful of art galleries, she had no idea what Trappers Cove offered for adults. "I'm not really the spa type."

"Said no one who's ever been to a spa." Cari waved off Danielle's comment with a flick of her fingers. "Take the money you'd spend on kid stuff and spend it on yourself."

Danielle gnawed on a ragged cuticle. Spa or no spa, some low-stress time at the beach sounded appealing—except that Trappers Cove oozed memories of happier times. Going there alone would only hammer home her loss. "I'd have that three-bedroom house all to myself. Seems like a waste."

Marie sighed. "Wish I could join you, but I volunteered to help at my kids' science camp."

"And I'll be in court for the rest of the month," Cari added.

"Sorry, Dani." Laurie flashed a crooked grin. "I promised to go to Spokane and help my sister with her new baby." She squeezed Danielle's knee, her eyes warm with sisterly affection. "But you should go. Really. It'll do you good."

Danielle straightened from her slump. Like it or not—and she damn sure didn't like it—thanks to Jason, she was stuck with the beach house rental. Maybe a few weeks away from home could help her figure out her next steps as a newly single mom. She stuffed a handful of popcorn into her mouth and chewed on the snack and her dilemma.

Finally, she nodded. "Okay. You're right. I'll go."

"You will?" Laurie pulled her in for a warm, squishy hug. "That's great, Dani."

Marie pumped a bejeweled fist in the air. "You go, girlfriend. Paint that cheesy beach town red."

Cari raised her glass. "Here's to fresh starts."

They all clinked glasses, then Danielle lifted her paperback from the coffee table. "So, are we gonna discuss the book or not?"

Laurie waggled her eyebrows. "Good thing we picked a murder mystery and not a romance. Let's talk bloody vengeance."

# Chapter Two

♥

Though it felt beyond weird to be here without her kids, Danielle realized—with a twang of mom guilt—she was almost enjoying her first day in Trappers Cove. The crowded main drag was so much easier to stroll without Noah and Olivia halting every few feet to beg for treats or souvenirs. Danielle slid through the crowd at her own pace, pausing to admire a display of blown glass vases and flip through a rack of colorful summer dresses. A reluctant smile tugged her lips upward as she inhaled the familiar scents of kettle corn, fish and chips, and salty sea. Maybe two weeks of this would do her some good after all.

Then she caught sight of her reflection in a shop window.

"Ugh." She'd smoothed her shoulder-length brown mane into a low ponytail, but the humid ocean breeze pulled tendrils loose and curled them into a wild frizz that totally clashed with her crisp outfit. She untucked her blouse from her linen skirt. Nope. Now she just looked sloppy.

Across the street, a pack of teen girls shrieked with laughter. The sight stabbed her with longing for her own daughter. Only thirteen, Olivia already possessed the sharp eye of a natural fashionista. She'd know exactly how to style Mom's outfit.

What would Olivia do? Danielle knotted her blouse at the waist. Better. Almost jaunty. Eyeing her reflection critically, she tugged the cloth lower to cover a soft roll of pale flesh. *Marie's right. I need sun.*

Her exposed middle rumbled. Well, she might lack company on this trip, but she sure didn't lack for culinary delights. During the school year, she'd opt for something healthy—an apple, perhaps, with low-fat string cheese. But this trip was about pampering her wounded heart and exhausted body. She scanned the street for the most deliciously sinful option. Snow cones, soft pretzels with gooey cheese sauce, pizza by the slice...

Bingo! Sandals slapping on the pavement, she made for her favorite gelato shop, Gelateria Paradiso. For as long as she remembered, trips to Trappers Cove included a visit to Salvatore, the opera-singing, silver-haired signore who always greeted her with a flirtatious "Ciao, bella." Exactly what she craved: sugar and sweet talk.

She entered the narrow storefront and took her place in line behind a family with three squirmy littles. Beneath bright posters of the Amalfi coast, she hummed along to the strains of Nessun Dorma while daydreaming of top-down rides on twisting, cliff-side roads above a sparkling blue sea.

"Ciao, bella." The unfamiliar voice snapped her reverie.

"Oh, uh," she stammered at the gorgeous young man smiling behind the counter. Dark, curly hair, wide, lush-lipped mouth, cleft chin covered with dusky scruff, and espresso-brown eyes that twinkled with flirtatious mischief. Broad shoulders filled out his tight black T-shirt beautifully.

Like a scene from a Fellini movie, everything around her slowed and blurred as his gaze slid down her body, then back up to her eyes and lingered for a long, breathless moment.

His glossy eyebrows flicked up in a cheeky salute. "Welcome to Paradiso, signora. Tell me, how can I serve you today?" With his ice cream scoop, he waved toward the Italian ices. "Something tart to soothe the heat? Limone or mandarino? Or perhaps something richer." He leaned onto the glass case and rested his perfect cleft chin on his fist. "Cioccolato fondente? Zabaglione? Tiramisu?" Rolling off his tongue, the words sounded far more like seductive foreplay than dessert options.

She swallowed hard and tugged her collar away from her suddenly sweaty chest. "Uh—so many choices. I can't decide."

His teasing smile widened, slow and sure. "Place yourself in my hands, bella. Just tell me how many scoops and let me surprise you."

She was helpless to resist. "Okay. You choose. Two scoops, please." She cleared her throat and found a bit of courage. "I place myself in your expert hands."

Was that a blush darkening his sculpted cheekbones? No, it must be a reflection from the deep red gelato he scooped into her paper bowl. He added a scoop of creamy white laced with ribbons of crimson, then raised a spray can and his eyebrows. When she nodded, he topped the bowl with a fluffy peak of whipped cream and handed it over, along with a plastic spoon.

"Tell me if I got it right." His dark gaze never left her face as she lifted a bite to her lips.

Subtle and creamy, hints of vanilla contrasted with a sharp burst of cherry flavor. "Wow."

"That's amarena. Bitter cherries with fior de latte." He gestured with a tilt of his chin. "Try the other."

She dug into the fruit ice. Tart and rich, the perfect foil. Mouth full and tongue a bit numb, she smiled and nodded.

"Frutti di bosco. Fruits of the forest. It's good, huh?" His flirtatious mask slipped a little, giving her a glimpse of the young man beneath, sweet and eager to please. And holy brain freeze, wouldn't she love to please him in return.

"The perfect combination. You are a true artist, signore." She glanced around the shop, grateful no new customers interrupted this surprise encounter. "But where's Salvatore?"

The brass bell above the door tinkled, and the old gent in question stepped through, thick silver hair gleaming, burly arms around a big Styrofoam cooler. He set his load on the counter, spread his arms wide, and flashed a mustachioed smile. "La bella Daniella!" He enfolded her in a warm hug and glanced over her shoulder. "But where's your family? I have your daughter's favorite right here." He patted the cooler.

The mention of her missing kids pierced her happy, sexy ice-cream dream. "I'm afraid they aren't coming this year. Jason and I, we—" No use boring her old friend with tales of Jason's infidelity, his coldness, his indifference. "We went our separate ways. The kids are with him in Southern California."

Salvatore's smile melted. He cupped her cheek in his broad, calloused hand. "Oh, cara mia, I'm so sorry."

Embarrassed by a wash of tears, she sniffled and lifted her cup. "Well, your new helper made me feel much better with his magic touch." Realizing how sexy that sounded, she quickly added. "With choosing flavors, I mean."

Salvatore chuckled. "My nephew loves the beautiful ladies, just like his old uncle. Come, sit. Visit with me a moment."

"Oh, but I haven't paid yet."

Salvatore patted her hand. "On the house." He led them to a little wrought-iron table near the front window and called over his shoulder, "Matteo, due espressi, per favore."

Sal glanced at his nephew. "My younger brother's boy. His papa died last March. Heart attack. Always working too hard. I told him to slow down and enjoy life. But would he listen to his big brother?" He raised his hands in a helpless gesture. "Matteo's been a great help in the shop since I lost my Giulia."

"Your wife? She's—"

Sal nodded and crossed himself. "Breast cancer. Terrible thing. If it weren't for Matteo, I woulda had to close the shop."

Danielle's heart wrenched, and she squeezed the old man's burly hand. "I'm so sorry, Sal. Giulia was a wonderful person."

Olivia and Noah would be heartbroken to hear they'd lost the tiny, bustling woman who always fussed over them when they came into the shop. "Beach nonna," they'd called her.

Sal dabbed his eyes with a paper napkin and jerked his thumb toward the counter. "Matteo's a good boy. A carpenter like my papà."

The good boy in question strode to their table, all six muscly feet of him. "Here you go, Zio Sal. Signora." He set down two steaming espressos.

Salvatore patted the table. "Sit, boy. Meet Danielle. She's been coming here for—how many years, bella?"

"Fifteen, at least." She regarded Matteo. How old was he, twenty-five? Faced with his glorious male beauty, she felt every year of her age—and then some.

Salvatore and his nephew leaned close across the table and muttered back and forth in Italian, their gazes flicking to her. Her knowledge of that language was limited mostly to food words, but divorziata was easy enough to understand. The two men straightened and faced her, Salvatore with a wide grin, Matteo with a shy one.

What happened to Mr. Suave?

"Danielle," Salvatore began, "would you do an old friend a big favor?"

"Umm." Her gaze skittered between them. "Sure, if I can."

"Tomorrow night, we are attending the Sons of Italy scholarship banquet. The food will be squisita." He kissed his fingertips. "But the old nonnas keep trying to set up Matteo with their daughters and granddaughters." He clapped his nephew's muscly shoulder. "If you come as our date, he can enjoy the party in peace. What do you say?"

Leaning onto his sculpted forearms, his fingertips inches from hers, Matteo added, "You'd be doing us a huge favor, Danielle. And he's right, the food is really good. Just dinner and a little dancing. Will you join us?"

How could she possibly say no to these two lady-killers? Between Sal's courtly, old-world manners and Matteo's sparkling, flirtatious gaze, she was a goner. Besides, her book club would approve. Hell, they'd stomp and pump their fists.

She smiled. "Sure, I'd love to join you."

"Stupendo!" Sal downed his coffee, gave her arm a gentle squeeze, and rose to greet incoming customers.

Upping the ante, Matteo took her hand and raised it to his lips. "Mille grazie, Danielle. You've saved me from the nonna mafia. I promise you'll have a good time." His warm, soft kiss on her knuckles triggered a cascade of happy shivers.

Flushed and stammering, she thanked him for the ice cream and watched him turn his dazzling charm on the next customer.

Could she...could they...maybe a summer fling?

She shook her head, dismissing the ridiculous notion. Just a nice young man flattering an old friend of his uncle's. Nothing to get excited about. Still, as she left the shop, she hummed along with Sal's Italian opera soundtrack, a giddy grin on her lips and a cocky sway in her step.

# Chapter Three

❤

"What do I wear to a Sons of Italy party?" Danielle muttered as, holding her phone aloft, she flipped through a rack of colorful hippie skirts in The Mermaid's Cave Gift Shop, Fashion Boutique, and Saltwater Taffy Emporium.

"Why not ask your gelato friend?" Cari asked from Danielle's phone screen and dug into her takeout carton. The most fashion-forward of their book club bunch, she'd joined Danielle's shopping expedition via video call during her lunch break.

"That'd make me look too eager." Danielle aimed her phone at a skirt in peacock blue, green, and purple, embroidered with feather designs and tiny mirrors. "Too much?"

"Not for a beach town. Besides, isn't that the point? You're breaking out of your drab routine." Cari gestured with her fork, loaded with dangling noodles. "Can't believe you didn't send a picture of this Italian stallion."

Danielle snorted. "Right. Shoulda snapped a pic for my friends' approval. That wouldn't be awkward at all." She flipped through a rack of tops until she found a floaty peasant blouse in emerald green, a perfect match for the skirt. "You like this?"

Cari whistled. "Fahncy! Try it on."

She carried both garments into the dressing room, propped her phone on the little shelf, and peeled off her boring blouse and skirt. "I have so few play clothes anymore. Just work outfits and gym clothes. That's sad, right?"

"It is sad, but you're taking steps to change that." Cari clucked her tongue. "Better get a new bra while you're at it. A woman with your assets should show them off, not squash them."

Danielle frowned at her reflection. "This is my favorite sports bra. It's comfortable." She turned to examine her profile. "I'll wear a better one tonight. Pokey wires and all." She pulled the blouse over her head, cinched the skirt's drawstring waist, and stepped back. *Wow!*

Cari gave a low whistle. "Oh, honey. That. Is. It. You look like a gypsy queen. What's her name, Esmerelda?"

Danielle tugged off her headband and fluffed her hair. "Didn't they hang her at the end of the book?"

"Not in the Disney version."

*Disney.* Just like that, her pleasure in the new outfit evaporated. She slumped onto the little stool in the corner.

"Oh, hey, I'm sorry." Cari clucked her tongue. "That was insensitive. Have you heard from your kids?"

"Just a few texts. They're having a great time." She blinked at the ceiling to hold back threatening tears. "Who am I kidding? Playing dress-up doesn't change anything. I'm still the mama drudge they'll come home to with stories about their cool new stepmom and their great vacation—"

Cari cut her off. "Jason's marrying that bimbo?"

She shrugged. "Not likely. She's the third new girlfriend since I finally kicked him out." She cracked a wry smile. "I almost feel sorry for her. I mean, spending all that money to impress her new boyfriend's kids, and he'll probably drop her in a few months."

"Yeah, but it still sucks." A buzz from Cari's end. "Judge is ready. Gotta go. But listen." She stabbed a finger at her screen. "Promise me you'll have fun tonight. I want a full report."

Danielle pasted on a brave smile and snapped a salute. "Aye, aye, Ma'am. Esmerelda out." She clicked off the call and surveyed her new look. The brilliant colors played up the contrast between her pale skin and dark hair and eyes. Would Matteo like it? She skimmed her fingertips along her exposed collarbone, imagining his plush lips there, the brush of his short, trim beard against her skin. *Mamma mia!* She fanned her flushed chest and throat, then slicked on rosy lipstick and snapped a few selfies.

She sent the best one to Olivia and Noah.

> **Going out to dinner with some new friends tonight. Hope you're having fun.**

Olivia's reply pinged seconds later.

> Pretty. Get dangly earrings, and don't wear those ugly sandals.

Noah's text came next.

> Mom's got a date? I'm telling Dad.

He added a wink emoji.

A wiser woman would tell her ten-year-old son it was just a potluck dinner with a bunch of strangers and the old gelato salesman. But in her heart of hearts, she hoped he would tell Jason. Maybe imagining her with another man would wipe that smug grin off her ex's face.

On her way back to the rental house, she passed Auntie Annabelle's Antique Attic, a sprawling shop that took up two adjacent houses. Bittersweet memories flashed across her mind's eye—trawling Trappers Cove's second-hand shops with her kids, hours of giggling as they tried on vintage hats, marveled at tin wind-up toys, and flipped through old comic books. Jason would grumble about "useless trinkets" and "worn-out junk" before leaving them to find a bar. It seemed with each passing year, he tried harder to spoil their fun.

And now he had. How could a rinky-dink beach town compete with Disneyland and Universal Studios? Though the shopping bags she carried weighed very little, her shoulders slumped—until she spotted something that jerked her upright.

Propped in the window behind cut-glass vases and creepy porcelain dolls sat a guitar. Not just any guitar, a gorgeous acoustic dreadnought, dark walnut with mother-of-pearl edging. How long since she'd played? Ten years? Fifteen?

Back in college, she was good enough to earn a hatful of tips on Saturdays in the little park behind Pike's Place Market, or in coffee shops near campus.

But her garage band fizzled, her coursework grew more demanding, and Jason claimed her free time. Then came marriage, work, and kids. Music receded into the background, just another thing she used to do.

She glanced at her fingers. Once upon a time, she'd sported short nails with sturdy callouses on her fingertips. Now she had a standard-issue gel manicure, just like all her suburban mom friends.

A slow smile stretched her lips. *New chapter. New beginning.* She squared her shoulders and strode into the shop. Half an hour later, she emerged with a vintage denim jacket, dangly beaded earrings, and the guitar. And she'd swear the sun shone a bit brighter as she sashayed toward home. Well, home for now, and she was damn sure going to enjoy it.

# Chapter Four

♥

As Danielle entered the low cinderblock building on Salvatore's arm, a blast of sensation slammed her: loud voices, laughter, and rich scents of garlic, cheese, fresh bread, and tomato sauce wafting from serving tables along the wall. Her stomach rumbled.

All dolled up for a party, the meeting hall was stuffed with big, round tables decked with flickering candles. On the low stage, Italian and American flags framed a D.J.'s table. People streamed through the entrance, greeting each other with hugs and backslaps. Kids dashed about, peeked from beneath tablecloths, and poked fingers into dishes. Mamas and grandmamas smacked little hands away from the feast. At a smaller corner table, old guys gesticulated over a dice game. Above the din, Dean Martin crooned, "Come back to Sorrento." Family, friends, food, fun—like all the best parts of Thanksgiving transplanted to June and sprinkled with Italian seasoning.

Danielle sighed. Her kids would love this. Over the years, she'd often wondered what it would be like to live full time in Trappers Cove. Tonight's party offered her a taste.

Salvatore tugged her toward a table in the center of the room and pointed to a folding chair.

"That's Matteo's jacket. Where's that boy gone to?"

Danielle scanned the crowd. "There he is." She hoped Sal didn't notice the fierce flush climbing her cheeks.

Backing through a side door and giving her a view of his broad shoulders flexing beneath a snug dress shirt, Sal's nephew carried an enormous, steaming pan, which he set on the buffet table. A petite nonna bussed him on the cheek, and another squeezed his biceps. As soon as his cargo was situated on its chafing dish stand, more grandmothers flocked to him like hungry sparrows, patting his cheeks and pointing to their own dishes of food.

Salvatore chuckled. "See? Those nonnas will tear him apart. Each one wants him for her own daughter or grand-daughter, and Matteo's too polite to chase them away." He nudged Danielle with his elbow. "That's your job, bella." He stuck two fingers in his mouth and let fly a piercing whistle.

Matteo's head snapped toward the sound. His brows flicked upward, and his smile widened.

Her heart skipped a beat or two, then thumped in time to his steps as he crossed the room. Despite the hands clutching at him, the hugs and backslaps, he kept his gaze trained on her—until a tiny princess in a poufy taffeta dress planted herself in his path, raised her arms, and demanded, "Up."

He scooped the toddler into his arms, smooched her fore-head, and carried her to the table where Danielle waited, barely breathing.

"Hi," the little girl announced with a serious expres-sion. "I'm Sophia. I'm this many." She held up two fingers, then three. "You're pretty." She patted Matteo's broad chest. "Down."

He raised a single eyebrow.

The little one heaved a comical sigh, shrilled, "Pleeeeeease," and was promptly set back on her feet.

As the child skipped into the crowd, Matteo took both of Danielle's hands. His gaze traveled over her body, leaving her slightly dizzy. If he was gorgeous yesterday in his black T-shirt, jeans, and apron, tonight he was simply spectacular in slim charcoal trousers, shiny loafers, and a crisp white dress shirt with sleeves rolled up to display strong forearms dusted with dark hair. His top two buttons were open, revealing a small silver medal against tan skin. Her fingertips itched to unbutton the next button, and the next.

His gaze met hers and held, his lips curving in a subtle, private smile. "Sophia's right. You're very pretty, Danielle." He pronounced her name with a panty-melting Italian accent, like some delicious dish.

*Mayday!* She sucked in a ragged breath and slid her hands from his soft grip. "Thanks. You're looking very dapper too."

She gave herself a mental smack. Dapper? What a dorky thing to say.

But Matteo's smoldering expression didn't falter. He moved closer, close enough to smell his subtle scent of sandalwood and sea air. Close enough to feel his breath tickling her ear as he whispered, "You're just in time. The nonnas were closing in."

Deep inside her chest, something fizzled like a snuffed candle. She'd misread the flicker in his dark eyes. He'd only asked her out as a shield against matchmaking matriarchs. For a split second, she considered excusing herself, claiming an upset stomach—not much of a stretch when faced with making a fool of herself over a younger man.

Then a skinny teen deposited a basket of steaming garlic bread on their table. Its tempting, yeasty aroma drew a rumble from Danielle's middle and triggered the memory of Cari's wise advice: "Promise me you'll have fun tonight." She couldn't break a promise to a friend. Besides, these two charming gents were counting on her.

Placing a hand on Matteo's firm shoulder, she rose on tiptoe and whispered, "You can count on me, bello."

"Mille grazie." He pressed a soft kiss to her temple. "Now, let's eat before all the best dishes are gone."

Flushed and flustered, she followed him to the buffet line and filled her plate with pasta, plus antipasti of marinated mushrooms, grilled vegetables, olives, cheese cubes, and paper-thin salami and prosciutto, along with peppery rucola salad and spinach-and-ricotta stuffed turkey involtini. Good thing her new skirt had a drawstring waist.

Back at the table, Salvatore filled her tumbler to the rim with red wine. "Local family makes this up near Westport. It's not Chianti classico, but it's not bad."

She sipped. "Not bad" was a huge understatement. Bold and complex, perfumed with berries and earth, the wine offered a perfect complement to the rich dishes before her. She'd tried most of the restaurants in Trappers Cove, but nothing came close to this feast. Their tablemates, two middle-aged couples and a retired fire chief, entertained them with town gossip and good-natured ribbing. Salvatore joined in, pointing his fork at the people being discussed. Matteo kept quiet, focused on the heap of food before him, but from time to time he nudged Danielle's leg and waggled his eyebrows, as if to say, "Isn't this delicious?"

After the chief's story about rescuing a cantankerous pet monkey from the church steeple, Matteo's hand closed softly over hers. "Seconds, bella?"

She blinked at her empty plate. Distracted by the genial company and Matteo's husky laughter, she'd hoovered down enough food for two dinners, maybe three. "Thanks, but no. If I eat any more, you'll have to roll me home."

The woman across from her asked, "So, Danielle, you Italian?"

"Partly. My grandfather's family came from Genoa. Dante Delfino was his name."

"Meraviglioso." The woman's husband pinched his wife's plump cheek. "See, Rosa? Matteo's found himself a nice Italian girl without your help."

Rosa gave her husband a shove, but the smile she gave Danielle glowed with genuine warmth.

Beneath the table, Matteo squeezed her knee, igniting sparks of pleasure that zinged up her leg. Why not play along? Just for tonight, she'd help her new friend by letting these matchmakers think they were a couple.

Rosa asked, "What do you do in Tacoma?"

"I'm a speech therapist for the school district."

Matteo leaned in, eyes alight with sincere interest. Or was he just that good at flattery and flirtation? "So, you help kids with lisps and stutters?"

She nodded. "Some of my students have difficulty with certain sounds, like L or R or TH. Others have speech delays or learning problems that affect their oral communication."

"Big kids or little?" Salvatore asked.

"Mostly little. With early intervention, they can make big improvements." She tapped her sternum. "Like me. When I was little, I couldn't say my S's. Other kids made fun of me."

Further explanation was interrupted when a tall, bony-faced gentleman stepped up to the podium to thank the chefs. A tiny, beaming nonna accepted a lavish bouquet for organizing the meal. She angled the mic down and rattled off a long list of names. "And thanks to Matteo, our muscle man, for carrying all the heavy stuff." She blew him a kiss, which he caught in his palm and pressed to his heart.

Danielle stifled a moan over his sheer adorableness. Though tonight didn't really count as a date, sharing this amazing feast with Matteo would definitely be the highlight of her solo beach trip.

"Before we start dessert," the MC continued, "you got ten more minutes to buy your raffle tickets. Remember, all proceeds go to the scholarship fund, so dig deep."

Salvatore pointed to a long table at the back of the stage. "Go take a look, you two. It's for a good cause."

Huh. Did her old friend have matchmaking inclinations too? People rose to stretch, and several moved toward the display of raffle prizes. Danielle slid through the crowd on Matteo's arm, their passage marked by whispers and pointing fingers.

"You're making quite an impression," he murmured. "Everyone's wondering who you are and how long you're going to stay."

"Just two weeks, I'm afraid. My kids have summer soccer league, and I have therapy appointments booked for July and August."

As they climbed the steps onto the stage, he pursed his lips and nodded slowly, seemingly deep in thought. "Tacoma's not so far away. I've been meaning to get up there and check out the antique shops."

"You're into antiques, Matteo?"

"Sort of. I upcycle old furniture, like this here." He pointed to a small table with a gleaming blue-green finish that allowed the wood's natural grain to shine through.

"Gorgeous." She ran her fingertips over the smooth surface. "Reminds me of my mother's sewing table."

His smile widened. "That's what it was, before I gave it a makeover. Open it."

She lifted the fold-out top. A galvanized tub sat in the cavity that once held a sewing machine.

"To hold ice and drinks." He pointed to the wooden lid. "You put your snacks here, and the cups go there."

"Matteo, this is brilliant." She squatted to see how he'd attached the tub.

He huffed and shoved a hand through his dark curls. "Nothing like helping kids learn to speak right. I mean, correctly."

Great, now she'd made him self-conscious. Swallowing a soft grunt, she pushed herself upright. "We all have our gifts. I lack your artistic talent."

"Artist? Hell, I'm a carpenter." From the open collar of his shirt, he pulled a small silver medal on a slender chain. "Saint Joseph, our patron saint. Gift from my grandfather."

"Was your dad a carpenter too?"

Another snort. Funny how he made that ungraceful noise sound so sexy. "Dad sold cars. Had a big, shiny dealership. Kept pressuring me to work for him—until he dropped dead from a heart attack at age sixty." He patted the tabletop. "I'll stick with carpentry."

Poor kid! He might laugh it off, but his wry half-smile betrayed a deep vein of hurt. She wanted to comfort this near stranger who made her pulse race, but she feared overstepping, so she settled for squeezing his shoulder, firm and solid beneath her hand.

Matteo wasn't so reticent, though. Not content with that skimpy contact, he pulled her in for a hug. Ignoring the flurry of whispers around them, he murmured against her hair, "Sorry to be such a downer. You're easy to talk to, Danielle. Thanks."

Fizzy warmth burbled up from her middle and filled her head with foolish thoughts. Fighting her reaction, she stepped back and pasted on a casual grin. "So, where do I get my raffle tickets?"

She bought twenty, depositing most in the jar in front of Matteo's ingenious bar cart, plus one each in a basket of romance books and bubble bath, as well as a picnic hamper filled with salami, cheese, and wine. When the drawing was held, she won the romance basket. A sign of good things to come? Or solitary nights curled up with a book? A cute young woman won Matteo's table, dammit.

Who was she kidding? With dozens of pretty young girls vying for Matteo's attention, there was no way he'd choose her company over theirs. Time to make a graceful exit before she made a fool of herself.

While he hauled the lucky winner's prize out to her car, Danielle thanked Salvatore for a wonderful evening, then shook hands with the rest of their tablemates and retrieved her wrap and purse. Returning to her side, Matteo pinned her with a puzzled frown. "You can't leave yet. You haven't had dessert."

"Dessert?" She patted her overstuffed tummy. "Where would I put it, in my purse? I had a wonderful time, Matteo, but I should get back home before—"

He leaned in close and whispered, "There's dancing too, and if you go, the nonnas will pounce." He ran his hands up and down her arms. "Please stay, bella. Dance with me."

The lights dimmed, and someone switched on a by-God disco ball above the dance floor. Its glittery shine transformed Matteo's dark eyes into a bewitching night sky.

"Well, I suppose..." She wet her lips as she draped her belongings over the chair back. She hadn't danced with a man since a stilted two-step at her wedding. Lately, she only hit the dance floor with tipsy women friends at concerts and parties. But now, Matteo was holding her hand, walking backward toward the dance floor where couples young and old swayed to "Volare."

He pulled her into his arms, his right hand between her shoulder blades, his left gently cradling her palm. For a moment that felt like forever, they stood beneath the spinning lights, gazes locked. His eyebrow quirked up. "Are you ready?"

She sucked in a breath, then nodded.

Away they glided. Maybe it was the wine, but it seemed her feet didn't quite touch the ground as Matteo guided her around the floor in swirling arcs. She was dimly aware of stares and whispers from the growing crowd of dancers. When the song ended, he spun her out and back, so she landed against his chest.

"You're a great dancer, Danielle." His soft kiss on her forehead sent giddy echoes through her whole body.

"That was all you, Matteo." Movement over his shoulder caught her eye—a trio of pretty twenty-somethings tittering at the dance floor's edge. Two of the girls shoved the third forward. "Incoming," she whispered.

Without releasing her, he glanced at the intruder, then pressed his forehead to Danielle's. "Can I kiss you?"

A flurry of sensations blanked her brain—the warm press of his skin, his woodsy scent, his breath whispering over her lips. Too stunned to speak, she nodded.

He captured her chin between thumb and forefinger and held her gaze for a moment, until his dark lashes fluttered down, and he closed the distance between them. His lips brushed hers, feather-light, and pressed softly at each corner of her mouth, which opened on a sigh. *Sweet Jesus*. When had she ever been kissed like this?

"Mmm," he hummed against her. His breath smelled of Chianti. He pressed her closer, hand splayed at the small of her back, and kissed her again, a long, voluptuous caress. She wound her arms around his neck and arched into his embrace, moaning helplessly as the tip of his tongue traced her lower lip.

"Madonna," he murmured. Beneath half-lowered lids, his eyes shone dark and molten.

A sharp whack on his shoulder shattered the moment. "Basta così," an older man scolded. "There are kids here. Go home if you're that arrapato."

Matteo threw his head back and laughed. "Means horny," he explained. "Sorry, bella. Your beauty is intoxicating. I got carried away." He pressed another kiss to the shell of her ear. "Will you forgive me?"

Face aflame, she nodded. "Should we go?"

He loosened his hold, once again taking her right hand. "As much as I'd like to get you alone, I'm enjoying dancing with you. Give me just one more?" As if on cue, the D.J. began a Sinatra tune.

She searched the dance floor for the giggly girls, but they'd disappeared into the crowd. The lights shifted to a rosy hue. Matteo swayed her slowly, keeping a safe distance this time, but the air between them crackled with electricity. Could the others see how she flushed and bloomed at his touch? They must have noticed because at each turn, eyes followed their movements, and murmurs trailed behind them.

"I think I'd better sit down," she told him when the music faded. "I'm feeling a little woozy."

On their way back to their table, they passed the girl who'd hoped to dance with Matteo. She muttered under her breath, but when Matteo gave her a dismissive wave, she raised her volume. "Cradle robber."

Danielle went rigid with indignation. *Jealous bitch.* The girl was right, though. Matteo was at least ten years her junior, maybe more. She must look ridiculous, making out with a much younger man in front of a roomful of strangers. The rosy cloud she'd been floating on a moment ago deflated, dumping her back to earth with a painful thud.

She squeezed his hand. "Matteo, I'm really tired. I think I'll head home."

Those mesmerizing dark eyes saw right through her lie. "Don't worry about Bianca. She's crazy, a real shit stirrer. Nobody listens to her."

She reached for her purse, dangling from the back of her chair. "Honestly, I had a wonderful time, but I'm ready for some quiet."

He hovered behind her, far too close for clear thinking. When she reached for her wrap, he unfurled it and draped it over her. His hands settled on her shoulders, a warm, heavy weight that kept her rooted in place. His breath stirred her hair. Finally, he sighed. "Okay. If you want to go, let me walk you home."

"No, really, I—"

"Too many drunk tourists out on a warm night like this. Please, bella. Let me see you to your door." His broad palms kneaded her tense shoulders. "Uncle Sal will give me hell if I don't."

Just then, Salvatore returned to their table holding a plate piled high with pastries. "What's this? Leaving before dessert?" He lifted a cannolo to her lips. "Stella Giusto made these. You'll never taste anything better."

"She's tired, Zio," Matteo interjected. "I'm gonna take her home."

Salvatore's expression of dismay smoothed into a knowing grin. "Ah. Okay, then. You two lovebirds go on home." Grasping her shoulders, he kissed both her cheeks. His mustache tickled. "I hope to see you soon, Danielle."

She nestled under Matteo's protective arm as they wound through the crowd. Outside, the cool evening air carried the ocean tang, more noticeable now that the Belgian waffle and kettle corn vendors had shut down for the night. Just as Matteo had predicted, boisterous tourists filled Main Street, roaming from one bar to the next. He kept his arm around her shoulders until they reached her rented cottage, only releasing her when they climbed the porch stairs, and she fished in her purse for the key.

"Nice place," he remarked. "I can see why you keep coming back."

"Yeah, well." She opened the door. "It's not the same without my kids."

According to Marie and her other divorced friends, the quickest way to get rid of a guy was to mention your offspring. But Matteo stood his ground, a dreamy smile on his face. "I'll bet you're a wonderful mama."

"How can you tell?"

He shrugged. "I dunno. You've got"—he waved a hand as if wafting smoke—"this caring aura. You're a very loving person."

"You can tell that from just one kiss?"

He shuffled closer. "One spectacular kiss." Closer still. "Fireworks, bella."

*Oh God, he's going to kiss me again. And I really, really want him to.*

His eyes glowed with the promise of passion. But instead of kissing her, he pressed his forehead to hers and chuckled. "And the fact that you'd go on a blind date with an old man and a stranger. That was a very sweet thing to do, Danielle. Thank you."

Disappointment tinged her sigh of relief. Better not think about how marvelous it would feel to kiss him again, how he'd taste, how he'd hold her, caress her...

She gave her head a little shake. "It was my pleasure, Matteo. I enjoyed that glimpse of the real town. You know, beyond the tacky shops." *Oops!* "I don't mean your shop, of course."

He tucked his chin and flashed a wry smile. "Yeah, Main Street's pretty damn tacky in summer. But there's a lot more to the town than tourist traps." His brows flicked up, and he seized her hands. "Let me show you, Danielle."

"Show me what?"

"The real Trappers Cove."

She chuckled. "I've been coming here since you were—" In high school? Elementary school? The thought landed like a rock in a puddle, splattering her dreams with muddy reality. "Anyway, I've seen Trappers Cove from top to bottom. The beach too."

"You've only seen the façade. Let me show you the real deal."

"I don't know, Matteo. You're so"—she waved her hand, taking in his gorgeous frame from top to bottom—"young, damn it."

He tilted his head. "Ah, the age thing. Okay, I'm thirty-one. You?"

She gulped. She'd never worried much about the passage of time. As her Italian nana said, you're as old as you are.

Useless to fret about it. But tonight, she wished she could turn back time for these two weeks, so she could be with Matteo without feeling so damn foolish.

She squared her shoulders. "I'm forty-two."

He stroked her arm with the back of his forefinger. "A woman in full bloom."

Her knees wobbled. Either he was joking, or he was a true seduction artist. She searched his dark gaze and found no mockery there. Maybe it was an Italian thing. Europeans held more appreciation for mature beauty, right? Or maybe he had a weird mama fixation?

*Who cares? I have two weeks to myself. Might as well enjoy them to the fullest.*

"All right, then. I'd love to see the town through your eyes, Matteo."

He grinned like a kid at Christmas. "Yeah? That's great. I have to work for Uncle Sal in the afternoon, so we can start with breakfast. Pick you up at seven?"

"In the morning?"

His thumbs teased her palms, massaging in slow, sensuous circles. "Put yourself in my hands, dear lady. I promise you'll have a good time."

# Chapter Five

♥

Danielle was still nervously fiddling with her hair when Matteo rapped on her door the next morning. The coastal wind had picked up overnight, and nothing spoils a flirtatious smile like hair stuck to your teeth. With a huff, she tucked an elastic band into the pocket of her red sundress, fluffed her wavy mane, and opened the door.

Her breath caught. Mamma mia, what a gorgeous man.

He leaned on one elbow, the very picture of beachy casual in slim knee-length shorts and a faded chambray shirt with rolled sleeves. His short, dark scruff framed a languorous smile.

"Good morning, bella. How beautiful you are this morning."

"Grazie, Matteo." Might as well use the dozen words of Italian she'd learned from her grandparents. Chalk it up to role-playing. While she was here, she was la bella Danielle, woman of mystery, pretend girlfriend to a gorgeous, much-too-young charmer. The dull realities of her life would return soon enough.

"Hope you're hungry," Matteo said as she locked up. "Callie's café has the best frittata."

"Frittata? Is everyone in this town Italian?"

He chuckled. "Lots of Croatians too. They make the best pasta fazool, but don't tell Uncle Sal I said that."

"Your secret's safe with me." She nudged his arm. He reached for her hand and, when she nestled into his soft grip, interwove his fingers with hers. That simple touch thrilled her nearly as much as last night's breathless kiss. What was his secret? Must be some powerful Italian sex juju.

With the tourists still snoozing in their motels, RVs, and rental cabins, Main Street was as quiet as an abandoned movie set. They passed a candy shop boasting "The Best Fudge in the Universe," a custom T-shirt vendor, and Souvenir Galaxy, all closed up tight. Callie's Coastal Café was still dark, but the tempting scents of bacon and coffee beckoned. Matteo tugged her down an alley to a back door propped open with a brick. "After you, my lady."

A narrow hallway led past the kitchen to a small dining room filled with chatting, munching customers.

Matteo pulled out a chair at the last empty table. "In summer, Callie saves this room for locals. Otherwise, we'd never get a seat."

A gum-cracking older woman with a welcoming smile stepped up to their table, an order pad at the ready. "Morning, gorgeous. Who's your friend?"

"Callie, meet Danielle, an old friend of Uncle Sal's."

Callie looked her up and down, then nodded her approval. "Glad to meet you, hon. What'll you have?"

Matteo leaned in close and lifted a single eyebrow. "You trust me, bella?"

"Absolutely."

He grinned up at Callie. "We'll have garden frittata, sausage, sourdough toast, and—coffee?"

Danielle nodded.

The frittata was a revelation: fluffy, cheesy eggs studded with onion, peppers, spinach, broccoli, mushrooms, and swirled with garlicky pesto. The sausage was Italian, spicy and scented with fennel seed. The toast was crisp, the coffee strong.

While they ate, Matteo waved and nodded to the other diners. "Hal's the mayor. That's his son, a teacher at the elementary school." He gestured over his shoulder. "Janice owns an art gallery and does those paint-and-wine parties. Out of season, she runs an art program for kids." A nod toward the corner. "Marquetta, the librarian, and her wife Zora—she runs the crystal shop. Pretty good fortune-teller. Told me I'd find fulfillment here in Trappers Cove."

"And have you?"

He quirked a mischievous smile. "Not yet, but things are looking up."

A thrill of anticipation skittered down her spine, right to her long-neglected lady parts.

After breakfast, he asked, "You mind a walk? Next stop's about a mile away."

She glanced down at her flat espadrilles, glad she hadn't chosen cuter, taller shoes. "A walk would be great."

They strolled through town toward the paved promenade, separated from the beach by grass-covered dunes. Only a few figures dotted the wide, flat beach at this early hour: old folks taking their daily constitutional, damp dogs galumphing after thrown sticks, and a few hopeful fishermen gazing seaward. The surf whooshed softly in and out, sheening the packed sand like a mirror.

"Nice to get out before the crowds," he commented as they strolled. "Summer keeps us so busy, I almost forget how beautiful it is."

She stopped at a bench to extract a pebble from her shoe, then laced her hands behind her head and leaned back on a sigh. "How does the song go?" She hummed a line, then softly sang, "Mother, Mother Ocean..." Of course, Matteo was too young to appreciate Jimmy Buffett.

But it seemed he wasn't too young to appreciate her, judging by his soft smile as his gaze drank her in from head to toe.

How long had it been since an attractive man noticed her, much less caressed her with his eyes? Flushed with a mixture of pleasure and embarrassment, she directed her gaze to the shimmering horizon. "So peaceful. If I lived here, I'd never let a day go by without visiting the beach."

"Why don't you?" Matteo sat beside her, his shoulder warm and firm against her bare skin.

"Why don't I what?"

"Live here."

Reality, that merciless bitch, jabbed her ribs.

"My kids. They're pretty rooted in Tacoma." The family counselor she'd consulted during the divorce stressed the importance of keeping the kids' lives as normal as possible. Their needs trumped her fantasies of a fresh start.

Matteo nodded. "Well then, you should visit more often." Extending his hand, he pulled her to her feet with a sturdy tug that knocked her off-balance.

She landed with her palm against his broad, warm chest. Heat infused her face as she stumbled back. "Um, yeah, I'd like to. But between my work and the kids' lessons and sports, it's hard to find the time."

His gaze dropped to the pavement.

*Change the subject, quick!*

"Nice of them to put these benches here."

"They're memorials." He pointed to a bronze plaque on the seat back. "To folks who lived and died here."

The plaque read, *In memory of Carlotta Agnesi, 1909-1992. Beloved wife, mother, friend, and maker of the best damn cioppino in Washington State. She loved this spot best of all.*

Danielle whistled. "Eighty-three years. Think of all the changes she saw in her lifetime."

"She lived longer than most. Lots of these plaques are dedicated to fishermen lost at sea."

As they strolled on, she calculated. She was already halfway to eighty-three, and how much time had she spent doing things she loved, in places she loved?

Matteo pointed toward a white tower rising above a stand of wind-sculpted cypress. "Gull's Point Lighthouse. Best view in town." He turned onto a path worn through scruffy brush.

"It's been ages since I visited the lighthouse." She pointed to a sign on the wooden gate. "Too bad. It's closed until noon."

Grinning, Matteo motioned her through. "Not if you know the keeper." He knocked on the door of the neat little cottage at the stone tower's base. It swung open to reveal a burly, ruddy-faced man with a grizzled jaw and bright, laugh-crinkled eyes. He ran a hand over his close-cropped ginger hair.

"Well, now, Matty-me-boy. You said you were bringing a friend. You didn't tell me it was a beautiful lady." He enveloped Danielle's hand in his calloused paws. "Fred Gallagher, at your service. Come in, come in." His hazel eyes twinkled, and his Irish brogue thickened. "Will you two be wanting the tour, or just the view?"

Matteo cocked an eyebrow in a silent question. While Danielle enjoyed an Irish accent, it was Matteo's deep voice she wanted to hear more of—wanted to bathe in, if she was honest with herself.

She linked her arm with Matteo's. "View, please."

Matteo's smile shimmered with sexy mischief as he covered her hand with his own.

"Right, up we go." Fred led them past a ticket counter and up a tall spiral staircase. Their footsteps echoed as they passed doors to the storage rooms and lighthouse keeper's quarters. At the top, a metal door clanged open. "Hold on tight, now.," Fred warned them. "It gets mighty windy up here."

Seen from below, the lighthouse tower hadn't seemed terribly high, but when she stepped onto the metal platform, dizziness seized her. She grasped the cold iron railing, rough with peeling paint. Wind whipped her hair and made her eyes water.

As if sensing her budding panic, Matteo stepped behind her and wrapped his arm around her waist. "I won't let you fall, bella," he murmured into her ear, and the goosebumps that bloomed over her skin had nothing to do with acrophobia.

Their guide settled against the wall, lit a cigarette, and launched into a story. "Out there." He pointed toward a cluster of rocky islands rising above the surf. "That's where it appears when the moon is full."

Matteo's chuckle rumbled against her back. "The ghost ship?"

"Aye. The Ivanova. Ran aground in 1822, coming back from Alaska with a cargo of furs. Everyone aboard perished. But when the moon is full, ye can still see her, a ragged ship with glowing sails. And down below," he pointed at the tower's base, "the captain's widow paces the shore, a spyglass in her hand, watching for her husband's return."

Danielle shivered, imagining the ghostly widow, forever searching the horizon for her lost love.

Matteo whispered, "He's probably making it up."

Fred snorted. "I heard that. Just you come back when the moon is full. See if you don't feel something."

Matteo's arm tightened around her middle. She damn sure felt something now, something powerful and a bit scary. She shivered again, despite the heat of his body pressing against hers from shoulders to knees.

Taking his cue, Fred cleared his throat. "Well then, I'll leave you lovebirds to it. Close the door when you come down. Don't want the seagulls shitting on the stairs."

"Romantic, isn't he?" Matteo nuzzled her hair, and the soft scrape of his beard on her cheek did funny, delicious things to her core. "Just imagine how it was in the old days when the lightkeeper held so many lives in his hands."

"Could we step back from the edge? I'm getting a little dizzy." Truthfully, it was Matteo's nearness more than the height that knocked her off-balance, but he didn't need to know that.

"Sure, bella. I want you to feel comfortable." He shifted to the wall and extended his arm.

She nestled beneath it and let the truth spill out—because why not? Soon, she'd return to her daily grind and never see this kind, flirtatious young man again.

"I am comfortable with you, Matteo. It's strange, since we met two days ago, but..." She shrugged. It didn't make sense, but this ease she felt in his company was as real and solid as this stone tower.

He nodded, his cheek against her hair. "Yeah, I feel it too. Some things you can't explain. They just are." He pressed a kiss to her temple.

Throwing caution to the stiff, coastal wind, she raised her chin and met his gaze.

He cupped her jaw in both hands, dark eyes sharp, as if he could see right through her fear, right to her galloping heart. His plush lips pressed to hers for a long, sweet moment. Pulling back, he threaded his fingers into her hair. "More?"

She nodded, and with a soft, hungry sound, he took her mouth in a luxuriant kiss. She relaxed into his hold, parting her lips to welcome the velvet heat of his tongue.

She'd forgotten how intoxicating it could be, this rush of desire washing through her like an incoming tide.

He slid one hand between her shoulder blades and splayed the other on the small of her back. He broke the kiss long enough to murmur her name, then pressed her to the wall, his strong arms cushioning her. A hard, hot ridge nudged her belly.

Must be the sea air, the dizzy height—because this was not her, this wanton woman groping and groaning atop a tower for the whole world to see. Her breasts ached for his touch, and her core throbbed in time with her racing heart.

With a soft chuckle, Matteo grasped her arms and stepped back. "Wow. That was—wow." Ignoring the erection straining against his zipper, he tenderly stroked her cheek with the back of his fingers. "I apologize, bella."

"Don't apologize." She grasped his hand and kissed his palm. "It's been a long time since anyone kissed me properly. You are"—she sighed—"a wonderful surprise, Matteo. Thank you."

His gaze danced over her face, and his kiss-swollen lips parted in a wicked smile. "You like surprises, Danielle?"

She bit her lip and nodded.

"Good to know." He glanced toward the open door. "But I can't entertain you properly up here. Shall we go down?"

Her imagination sprinted toward steamy possibilities, but she forced her gaze upward, to his sparkling dark eyes and not the sweet temptation below his belt. "Yes, let's."

He didn't speak much on their walk back to town, but he held her hand, his grip easy and loose. The ocean breeze cooled her fevered skin, but her mind raced ahead. Where were they headed? Back to her place for a tumble in her rented bed? Nothing had ever sounded more enticing. Or more terrifying.

With quick, darting glances, she sipped at Matteo's beauty—the wind ruffling his curly dark hair, the play of light and shadow across his smooth brow and sharp cheekbones, his graceful gait.

For eighteen years, Jason had been her only lover, his body as familiar as her own. She'd chalked up his declining libido to the passage of time, to their busy schedules, to the inevitable cool-down that came with knowing your partner so well. Turns out, she hadn't really known him at all. And his libido was as frisky as ever, just directed elsewhere. The day his now ex-girlfriend called to drop the bomb about their affair was the day her sex drive closed up shop. Shutters down, lights out, doors locked.

Until Matteo.

When they reached her corner, he spun and clasped her hands. His broad chest rose and fell while his eyes searched her face.

Panic tightened her throat. This was it—crunch time. He was going to ask her back to his place, or to hers, and she had no freakin' idea what to say.

He glanced heavenward and blew out a long breath. "Bella, I'm in a tough spot right now."

Something inside her deflated. He was groping for a way out.

He stepped off the sidewalk to make room for a family with four bouncy kids heading toward the beach. The littlest child bonked into Danielle with his enormous inflatable unicorn. "Sorry!" he chirped.

Still holding her hands, Matteo drew her to a patch of shade beneath a cluster of anemic palm trees and flashed an adorable, shy grin that crinkled the corners of his eyes. "Danielle, I really like you, but I don't want you to feel like I'm pressuring you to do something you're not ready for."

*"I'm ready!"* her id hollered and waved like an over-excited second grader.

Matteo twined his fingers with hers. "Unfortunately, Sal needs me this afternoon, and I'm driving him to Aberdeen tonight. How about tomorrow? We could have a picnic lunch on the beach. There's a special spot I'd love to show you." He dipped his head and nuzzled the sensitive crook of her neck. "Are you still up for it? Or have I scared you off with my grabby hands?"

The heat of his breath scrambled her brain. No doubt about it, he wanted her. And she wanted him so badly her teeth ached.

She sucked in a deep breath. "I'll bet you get a lot of single women tourists throwing themselves at you."

He shrugged. "A lot of women flirt. Doesn't mean anything." He rested his forehead against hers. "I collect drawer pulls, and doorknobs, and picture frames, not women."

She pressed her lips together and dropped her gaze to their joined hands. This guy definitely earned an A-plus in handholding. Never had such a simple act felt so intimate, so sensual. The way his thumb traced arcs across her knuckles made her imagine what those hands could do on her bare body, stretched out on her king-size bed, the sea breeze lifting the curtains while his palms glided over her breasts...

Her common sense made a last, futile stand. "Matteo, I'm old enough to be your—"

"No." He squeezed her hand. "You're not. Though you are old enough to be my sexy babysitter." His chuckle rumbled deep in his throat. "Every guy's fantasy."

She spluttered a laugh, and he joined in. "Last night, you helped me by pretending to be my date. That was a sweet, generous thing to do. But I'm not pretending today, Danielle." He released her. "What do you say? Lunch tomorrow if I promise to keep my hands to myself?"

Swallowing hard, she nodded, even though she'd much rather have his hands all over her. And she suspected that's exactly where they'd be tomorrow night.

"Great." A wide grin lit his face. "I'll meet you at noon." He pecked her lips, then turned and jogged toward town, leaving her to stumble back to her cottage, her heart tripping like a sprinter's.

Inside, she collapsed onto a wicker chair by the front window and grinned into the distance, slowly shaking her head. She reached for her phone to share the news with her book club friends, then paused, finger poised over the screen.

Soon, she'd share the happy news. Cari, Laurie, and Marie would applaud her audacity. But for now, she'd keep this sweet surprise to herself, polishing it like a secret jewel, something to keep her warm in colder days to come.

# Chapter Six

♥

When Matteo knocked promptly at noon, Danielle squeaked like a cat toy, gulped a deep breath, and quick-stepped to the door. There he stood, leaning on the frame, a knowing smile on his handsome face. Such a sexy, relaxed pose. Did he rehearse in front of a mirror?

"Hi." She pecked his cheek. "Come in."

He set his backpack on the table by the door. "I like what Mary's done with the place." He gazed around at the cushy couch and white canvas armchairs, the bright pillows embroidered with sea creatures, the porthole mirror above the brick fireplace, and the nautical knickknacks.

"You know the landlady?" she asked.

"Limoncello gelato in a sugar cone and espresso doppio." He grinned. "I doubt there's a full-time resident Sal hasn't introduced me to. Hey." He stepped around the counter into the kitchen. "That table's one of mine."

"Really? I love this piece." She trailed her fingertips over the tabletop's little blue and green tiles scattered with gold like glints of sunlight on water.

"This started as doors from an old dining room hutch." He stroked the blue-tinted wood as if caressing a lover. "Picked up the tiles from an art shop going out of business. Serendipity, eh?"

She nodded. "It's gorgeous." Like its creator, the table had a beautiful surface and surprising depth. Original too. An idea snapped into place. "That's what you should call your shop."

"Pardon?"

"Serendipity. Perfect name for what you do." She flushed, aware he could take that in more than one way. "With old furniture, I mean."

He chuckled. "I'll keep that in mind if I ever get a shop of my own. For now, I'm doing fine with word of mouth." His brows drew together as he patted the tabletop. "Not looking to set the world on fire. I just want to make good quality pieces."

Oh, crap. Did he think she was criticizing him? She brushed the awkward moment aside by fluffing the full skirt of her navy sundress. "I wasn't sure what to wear."

When he faced her again, the scowl was gone, replaced by a crooked grin. "You look gorgeous. As long as you can climb over rocks in that, you're golden." He gestured toward the backpack. "Gourmet picnic for two. Better than braving the mob on Main Street."

"Not a fan of the tourist hordes?"

He shrugged. "Can't blame people for loving the beach. But I'd rather focus on you without shouting over the noise, you know?"

She ducked her head to hide her flushed cheeks. "Give me two secs to pack a few things." Back in the bedroom, she slid into sturdy Keds, rubbed sunscreen on her shoulders and across her nose, then packed her bag with a ball cap from her daughter's soccer team, a towel, tissues, a phone charger, a few Band-aids and antiseptic wipes...

"God, I'm such a mom." Too bad she hadn't packed condoms and lube for this trip, but honestly, the thought had never occurred to her.

Once again, they strolled toward the beach. The sun burned brighter today, and the wind had calmed to a soft breeze that lifted her hair and cooled her damp nape. Matteo kicked off his Vans and led her across the pebble-strewn sand, past lounging families, giggling kids, and dogs chasing sticks and frisbees, until they reached the water's edge, where he paused, his dark gaze trained on the horizon.

"I never get tired of this," he murmured. "Il mare. My ancestors have always lived near the sea. Fishermen, boatbuilders, traders—the tides run in our blood." Stepping behind her, he wrapped his arms around her waist. Her breathing slowed, soothed by the waves' whispered rhythm. Cool breeze at her front, warm man at her back, perfectly at peace.

His grip tightened. "How can it be, bella mia, that I never met you before? Every summer, I was here, and you were here. We must've passed on the street dozens of times."

That very question had danced in her head as she lay in bed last night, basking in the afterglow of Matteo's kiss. How could she have missed him—in the gelato shop, on the beach, in the stores on Main Street? Just an accident of time, a corner turned two steps ahead of him, a child's distracting cry, a husband's grumpy complaint.

She huffed a laugh. Until this spring, she'd been a married woman. Even if he'd caught her eye and flashed that molten smile, what could she have done about it?

"Come on." He stepped back and reached for her hand again. "Tide's starting to turn. We've gotta hurry to catch this spot. I don't want you to miss it." They strolled up the beach, pointing out sights along the way: a formation of pelicans diving with military precision, a joyful yellow Lab splashing into the surf, a trio of little boys giggling as they buried their dad in sand. A bittersweet pang pulled tears to her eyes. So many memories of happier days when her kids were small. But this was a happy day too. Her life had changed, but it wasn't over.

They reached a wall of stacked boulders. "We cross here," Matteo said while stepping into his Vans. "Better put your shoes back on." Holding her hips from behind, he boosted her onto a limpet-encrusted rock. She scrambled over the top and dropped onto a small, deserted cove, no bigger than half a soccer field, ringed by jagged, pine-topped cliffs.

"It's beautiful," she exclaimed. "All these years coming to Trappers Cove, I never knew this was here."

"Ivan's Hollow. Unless the tide is all the way out, you have to climb the rocks to get in. Every summer, some idiot drives through at low tide, parks too close to the surf line, and loses his truck to the sea." He dropped his backpack onto the sand and pulled out a checkered blanket. "You hungry?"

"Starving."

While she nestled her butt into the soft sand, Matteo set out paper plates and two foil-wrapped sandwiches. "Ali Baba's kebabs, the best on the coast. I wasn't sure which toppings you like, so I got them all on the side." He arrayed foil packets holding paper-thin slices of red onion, cucumber, tomato, shredded white cabbage, black olives, and slabs of feta cheese. A cardboard tub held garlicky tzatziki sauce, and another held spicy harissa. Cold cans of flavored seltzer water completed the feast.

"Yum!" She paused, bamboo spoon aloft. "Are you having garlic sauce on yours?"

"And onions. Don't worry, I brought mints for after, just in case." He waggled his eyebrows.

They loaded up their sandwiches and feasted, tossing bits of pita bread to the ever-increasing flock of seagulls who tap-danced just out of reach. When one got too aggressive, Matteo leapt to his feet and charged at the birds, flapping his arms like a deranged scarecrow. Danielle laughed so hard seltzer sprayed out her nose.

Chuckling, he dropped down beside her again. "We're at the top of the food chain, baby." He thumped his chest. "No one's stealing our kebabs."

She patted her middle and smiled. "Greasy, spicy, salty goodness. Brilliant choice, Matteo. Thank you." She stuffed their wrappers into the backpack and leaned back on her elbows with a contented sigh. "Seems you're always feeding me something delicious. You'll have to let me cook for you."

"I like that idea." He reclined on one elbow and twirled a lock of her hair around his forefinger. "What's your specialty?"

His smoldering gaze ignited a tendril of lust that meandered through her body and flared between her thighs. She fanned her skirt to hide her squirming. "Well, I make a pretty good coq au vin."

The corners of his lips inched upward. "It's a date. I'll bring the wine." He rolled away and dug into the backpack. "Speaking of—" He pulled out a leather-covered flask and two tiny metal cups. "Nocino. Walnut liqueur, good for the digestion. Uncle Sal swears by this stuff."

She took a cautious sip—nutty, with sweet spices, and not too much alcohol. "Delicious." She drained her cup, then stretched out, head pillowed on her folded arms, and watched cloud castles sail inland. The soft whoosh of surf and the press of midday heat soon had her eyelids drooping. Stifling a yawn, she rolled onto her side. "Don't want to fall asleep and end up stranded by the tide."

"I can think of worse fates." He held up a little tin. "Mint?"

"Subtle, aren't you?" Giggling, she took one and crunched it up.

"Well, I've only got two weeks to convince you." He popped a mint into his mouth, stretched out on his side, and grinned.

Oh, that minty, garlic-tinged, playful, seductive, beautiful smile. The contrast between dark, close-trimmed whiskers and plush, dusky-pink lips completely undid her.

She sucked in a breath and almost smoothed the tremor from her voice. "Convince me of what?"

"To give this a try." He pointed to his own chest, then to hers.

"You mean a little vacation fling?"

"No, bella. A woman like you could never be just a fling."

She snorted—probably not the reaction he was looking for. But instead of looking hurt, he chuckled. "Too cheesy, eh?"

"Just a little. But thanks for the compliment."

"So." He scooted closer on the blanket and rested a hand on her hip. "What do you say? Are you up for an adventure? You've got a ready-made escape clause."

Mere inches away, his nearness made it damned hard to concentrate. "What do you mean?"

"Two weeks. When it's over, you decide. If you got what you wanted, you leave me behind, knowing you made a lonely guy very, very happy." His hand slid oh-so-slowly down her thigh. "If you still want more, we'll figure out a way to make it work."

"Mmm hmm." The warmth of his palm burned through her skirt. "And if you don't want more?"

His voice dropped to a husky growl. "Oh, Danielle, I will definitely want more. Call me crazy, but when we danced, something inside me started to—I don't know how to describe it. Hum? Glow? Fizz?" One-handed, he bunched her skirt, baring her thigh. The sea breeze raised goosebumps on her exposed skin.

He nuzzled the sensitive crook of her neck. "You and me, we've got chemistry. Electricity. Magnetism." The soft scrape of his beard sped her pulse and melted her bones.

His fingertips skimmed over her upper thigh.

Just a little vacation fling. What difference could it possibly make? When it was over, she'd go back home, and everything would return to normal.

"Two weeks," she murmured and tugged his shirt loose from his belt. Her greedy hands skated over satin skin.

Maybe he was using her, a convenient distraction to keep the nonnas off his sculpted back, the horny single girls of Trappers Cove out of his silky hair. Even so, what he offered was far too tempting to resist. This gorgeous young man wanted her. The evidence thrust gently against her thigh—a hard, hot ridge of desire.

Heat pooled between her legs, pulsing, demanding. With a groan, she rolled atop him, her sopping panties pressed to his rough denim and splayed her fingers over his firm pecs.

His chest rose and fell beneath her palms. His lids lowered and his lips parted on a sigh as he grasped her hips and arched up against her sex. Back and forth he guided her, each slow pass over his erection shooting bright sparks of pleasure up her spine. Her breath stuttered. She was going to come any second now, and she wanted to feel him deep inside her as she tipped over the edge.

She fell forward and took his mouth in a sloppy, hungry kiss. "Do you have protection?" she murmured against his lips.

He gaped for a moment, then laughed. "Beautiful Danielle, as much as I want you, I don't want to get sand in your most sensitive places. And the tide's coming in. Let's find some-where more private and less gritty."

Wincing, she rolled off him. Thank God his brain cells were still firing, because hers were totally fried by lust. While she folded the blanket, he stuffed the remains of their feast into his backpack. He slid the straps over his shoulders and pulled her against him, belly to belly.

There it was again, that perfect balance of sensation: warm, firm body and cool ocean breeze. Soft brown eyes and hard, pulsing cock. Balanced on the sharp edge between risk and safety, delight and disaster, she could turn back now, or plunge ahead. But for just a moment, she rested here and breathed in rhythm with the sea. Whatever came next, she wanted to remember this moment.

She deserved this.

Feigning confidence she didn't quite feel, she cocked a hip and smiled. "You know, my place has a big, sand-free bed."

He bit his lip and grinned. "Does it now?"

"And the headboard has pretty carvings. Seashells, I think. Wanna see?"

"How can I resist?" Mischief sparkled in his eyes as he danced her backward. "Artistic furniture is my jam."

When her heels collided with the rock wall, she tottered and nearly fell.

His arms closed around her shoulders. "Careful. Wouldn't want to scrape that beautiful skin."

They stepped into their shoes and scrambled over the rocks. On the other side, Matteo grasped her waist and lifted her down, sliding her against his front in the process. He rocked his hips against her. Head lolling, she clung to him, lost in delirious pleasure.

"Dude," a voice rang out behind them. "Not in front of my kids."

"Oh, God." She buried her face in the crook of his neck and shuddered with mortified laughter. When her kids were little, she'd had to divert their attention from amorous couples on the beach. And now, here she was, dry humping her new friend as if no one else could see. How gloriously tacky. How wicked.

Blushing darkly, Matteo stepped back and waved at the gawking sandcastle builders. "Sorry, guys. We were just, uh..."

Memory served up an explanation she'd used with her own kids. "Dancing. We were dancing. Great castle, guys." She flashed them a thumbs-up, kicked off her shoes and stuffed them into her bag, then grasped Matteo's hand and trotted away. Seafoam tickled their toes as they ran along the water's edge. When the kayak rental place came into view, they turned toward town and slogged through slippery dry sand dotted with broken shells and driftwood.

They continued barefoot. The sand-dusted sidewalk felt good under her feet.

Matteo slung his arm around her shoulders and snugged her tight to his side. A few people heading for the beach greeted him by name as they passed.

"They'll think I'm your girlfriend," she whispered.

He squeezed her shoulder. "You are, bella."

Somewhere in the back of her lust-addled, sun-drunk brain, a warning bell jangled. But when they turned the corner toward her cottage, all thoughts of consequences evaporated like the early-morning fog.

At her front door, he took her hands, a solemn expression on his handsome face. "Danielle, are you sure want this?"

This sweet, horny, so-damn-young man was worried about rushing her. "Do you?"

He nodded slowly. "My bones ache from wanting you."

A fizzy sensation filled her, as if someone had lifted the top of her skull and poured in a bottle of champagne. "Me too." She unlocked the door.

# Chapter Seven

♥

It wasn't easy to unlock the cottage door with her mouth sealed to Matteo's and her left hand tunneling beneath his shirt, but she finally managed. He shrugged his backpack onto the floor, cupped her face in his broad, warm palms, and kissed her breathless. His velvet tongue teased her lips apart while he grasped her ass through her skirt and pulled her tight against him. Beneath his jeans, his cock stood at attention, a heated ridge of flesh against her belly.

For the past several years, she'd had to tease Jason's indifferent penis to erection with her hands and mouth, but Matteo was ready to go right now, and her pussy tingled with an urgency that edged toward pain. Mouthing a silent prayer of thanks, she fumbled with his belt.

"Easy, now." Matteo gently disengaged her greedy fingers from his buckle. "We're all sandy. Let's clean up first."

Her cheeks flushed hot. What a dork she was, mauling him like some clumsy, horny virgin. But his hypnotic gaze held no mockery, just desire so intense it made her insides vibrate. She took his hand. "A shower sounds great. This way."

As soon as they stepped into the bathroom, Danielle froze. Sunlight flooded through the skylight, glinting off the huge mirror. He was going to see her forty-two-year-old body in excruciating detail, every roll, every spider vein, every dimple. Nausea churned in her belly.

Her wide-eyed look of horror reflected in the mirror. So did Matteo's hooded gaze as he ran his hands down her arms, raising trails of goosebumps. "Look at you, Danielle. So beautiful, so lush..." He nuzzled her hair and inhaled its scent. "You're glorious."

She gulped and met his reflected gaze. Slowly, he unzipped her sundress and let it fall to pool at her feet.

Matteo's breath caught, then came out in a whoosh that stirred her hair. "Sei bellissima." His fingertips skimmed over the cups of her black lace bra before lowering the straps. With a soft, hungry grunt, he pressed a kiss to her shoulder, his hair tickling the crook of her neck. Her nipples contracted to sensitive peaks as he swirled feathery caresses over her breasts, down her stomach, along the flare of her hips, finally coming to rest on the tender insides of her thighs, mere inches from where she wanted him. Needed him. Now.

Of their own volition, her hips undulated in slow circles, but he made no move to lower her panties, content to trace the edges of the thin fabric. "That's it, Danielle. Dance with me. No one's ever moved with me like you do." At last, his fingertips whispered over her mound, drawing a shudder, then slipped beneath the elastic.

Oh, God—should she have shaved? Waxed?

Matteo pressed closer, his belt buckle cool against the small of her back. His hips rocked, a subtle sway that brushed his rigid cock over her ass and sent her pussy into a flurry of urgent contractions. With agonizing slowness, his fingers parted her throbbing folds and slid over the slick wetness inside. The shock of pleasure jolted her.

"A goddess." He stroked her, passing two fingers over her clit, then plunged them inside her slippery channel.

She jerked and gasped, but he held her firmly in place. "Look at me, bella."

With a ragged inhalation, she focused on their reflection. A rosy flush tinted her face and chest. Her marble-hard nipples strained against black lace. Her stomach rose and fell. And behind her, Matteo's heavy-lidded stare, his parted lips, his mussed hair. In a voice husky with desire, he murmured, "See how beautiful you are. Watch me make you come."

"But I want you—"

His fingers curled inside her, and lightning flashed up her spine.

"Soon, cara." He maintained a steady rhythm, light glides over her clit interspersed with strong thrusts inside. Her bones melted. The room blurred and swam around her. But she kept her gaze on his dark, burning eyes. "Give me this first," he murmured. "Let me see you come." He clutched her breast, kneading the sensitive flesh and brushing his thumb over her nipple.

"Matteo, I—" Her words dissolved into a high, keening cry as climax tore through her in wave after wave of electric bliss. He rode it with her, his eyes locked on hers, his hand gently caressing her until, too over-sensitized to continue, she finally squirmed free.

He brought his glistening fingers to his lips and licked them clean. "Mmmmmm. Deliziosa." He tugged his shirt over his head. "Now I need my skin against yours."

While she clung to the counter, still too wobbly to trust her legs, he unclasped her bra and let it fall, then peeled off her panties.

Insecurity gripped her, just for a moment, but there was no mistaking the desire flickering in his dark eyes. He wanted her, and that knowledge infused her body like a shot of sweet liquor, relaxing her tense muscles. She turned to face him, bare ass against the cool tile counter, and ran her hands over his chest.

She'd forgotten what this felt like: satin skin dusted with coarse hair, firm muscle, pounding pulse. She trailed her fingertips over his pecs and brushed her thumbs over each flat, brown nipple before following his tantalizing happy trail down to his belt. "Let's get you out of this," she murmured as she unfastened the buckle.

She slid the rough denim down, then hooked her foot in the waistband and shoved his jeans to the floor. He wore nothing underneath, and his cock sprang free, hard and thick, a glistening teardrop on the plump crown.

"Oh my." She raked her nails over his smooth flanks and the muscular curve of his ass. "You are glorious." With a hungry moan, she cupped his silky balls and stroked his shaft.

His eyes drifted shut, and his jaw relaxed on a shuddering sigh. His hips rocked toward her, his heavy cock gliding across her palm. With a hiss, he stepped back. "Shower first. I want you stretched out on your bed so I can get at all of you."

He cranked the faucet and tugged her beneath the steaming spray. Sand ran off their legs and feet and swirled down the drain. He squirted shower gel into his palm and stroked it down her arms, then slicked his hands over her breasts.

"So good," she murmured as she filled her palms with citrusy bubbles. Round and round she glided over the flare of his collar bones, his sculpted chest and broad back, his taut belly, the sexy hollow at the side of each hip. With soft purrs and moans, they explored each other—until she reached his cock. He allowed her one soapy stroke before pulling away.

"Baby, I want to come deep inside you, not in your hand. Can I do that?"

She nodded. Every nerve howled for more, but the wait would only increase their pleasure.

After rinsing, they continued their mutual exploration, patting each other dry with big, fluffy towels. He took extra care to blot the tips of her hair, now curling wildly from the damp heat. His gaze flicked to the bottle of lotion on the counter.

If he kept delaying, she was going to explode.

She grasped his hand and led him across the hall to the bedroom. A breeze lifted the filmy curtains, and laughter from the cottage next door drifted through the slightly open window. She moved to close it.

"No, leave it." He gently gripped her arm. "Let's make them jealous."

With Jason, she'd always taken pains to ensure the kids never heard their lovemaking. He kept mostly silent anyway, his motions mechanical, his face a stony grimace as he pistoned in and out of her. With Olivia and Noah in the house, she fought her natural tendency to sing out her pleasure. Not that she'd reached her peak all that often with her ex.

But Matteo invited her, even challenged her to get loud. How deliciously wicked. She fell backward onto the bed, pulling him down beside her.

With a sexy growl, he crouched over her and kissed her forehead, each closed eyelid, her throat, before savoring her mouth with soft brushes of his lips and teasing flicks of his tongue. She wound her arms around his neck to pull him closer, but he slid from her grasp. On hands and knees he descended, dropping kisses onto her shoulders, her sternum, and suckling deeply at each breast. Happy sparks flew from her nipples to her clit. She'd never been able to come from breast play alone, but if he kept this up, she just might.

He licked a tingling line down the center of her belly, circled her navel, and finally reached her mound.

"So lovely." He parted her thighs and settled between them. One finger lazily stroked her seam before sliding inside. He traced the edge of her inner lips with his fingertip, then his tongue.

A groan escaped her throat—a ragged, animal sound. She raked her fingers through his dark mane and pulled him tighter against her.

His sexy laugh rumbled. "You like that, bella?" He knelt beside the bed, grasped her thighs, and pulled her to him. His fingertips spread her wide—and then, nothing. She waited, heart thundering, but felt only the whisper of his breath. She lifted her head to peer down at him.

He gazed raptly at her pussy, a dreamy smile on his face. "Like a seashell," he murmured, softly caressing her coarse curls. "The prettiest part hidden deep inside, pink and shiny and delicate."

Her lover had the soul of a horny poet. She stroked his hair and very nearly blurted, 'I love you.'

Her heart squeezed at this moment of reckless stupidity. This wasn't love, just a bit of fun, a vacation fling. She mustn't let herself fall for the beautiful young man admiring her cooch, no matter how sweet his words, how skilled his touch. Their connection had an expiration date. She couldn't allow herself to forget that.

Until Matteo plunged his tongue between her folds, and her common sense was no help at all. Primitive need took over. There was only this moment, this man. His beard tickled her thighs while his fingers and tongue lifted her to dangerous, dizzying heights until she fell and soared all at once as bright, sharp pleasure blanked her mind and rocked her body. At last, she subsided against the bed, blissed-out and boneless.

His chuckle rumbled between her limp thighs. "Una dea—a goddess." He rose, swiped his glistening mouth on his forearm, and crawled over her like some great jungle cat, muscles shifting beneath golden skin, eyes glittering. He kissed her belly, her breasts, her throat, before plunging his tongue into her mouth. Her own scent clung to his beard. She'd marked him, and the knowledge flamed inside her. Despite two powerful orgasms, she craved more.

He rose onto his knees, still straddling her, and his cock bobbed upward, ruddy and thick, its rosy crown slick with pre-cum. She reached for him.

"Just a moment." He climbed off the bed and trotted, gloriously naked, back toward the bathroom. "Condoms in my jeans."

He returned with a fistful of foil packets and a mischievous grin. "Take your pick, beauty."

A giggle burbled up. She hadn't used a condom since those early days with Jason. She grabbed a packet without looking, ripped it open, and extracted a slippery, hot-pink disk that smelled of strawberry bubble gum.

Matteo held out his hand, but she shook her head. "Let me." While he stood beside the bed, she rolled the thin sheath over his pulsing shaft, shiny cartoon pink over deeper, rosy skin. She feathered kisses over the soft, fuzzy sack beneath. The dusky skin contracted at her touch.

His fingers threaded into her hair, drawing her back. "That feels so good, but I want to be inside you."

She lay back, and with a rumbling moan, he crawled over her. Supporting his weight on one hand, he positioned himself at her entrance. The contact sent delicious shivers through her whole body. He held her gaze as he slowly pushed inside. Her inner muscles resisted at first, but the steady pressure opened her to him, making each unhurried thrust more exquisite. With a raw groan, she wrapped her thighs around his hips to pull him even closer.

He set a steady rhythm, gliding in and out while raining kisses everywhere he could reach.

Her breath came in shallow pants. White-hot pleasure swelled inside her.

Eyes closed, he drove into her faster, harder. He dropped still lower, forearms bracketing her head, his chest and belly pressed to hers, magnifying the heavenly pressure building throughout her body until another blinding climax whirled her away.

"Ah, bella," Matteo groaned into the crook of her neck as his cock pulsed inside her.

Ribs heaving, he collapsed over her, a warm weight that grounded her until her senses returned.

"Oh, God," she gasped, fingers tangled in his hair. "That was—you are—sweet Jesus."

Still panting, he grinned. "We're so good together, Danielle."

She brushed a stray curl from his glistening forehead and pulled him down for a kiss. They were good together. Spectacular. Sex with Jason had never felt this amazing. And afterward, he always rolled off and took a shower, leaving her alone in their damp bed. Fastidious, he was, and impatient with post-sex cuddles.

Matteo slowly withdrew, plucked tissues from the box on the bedside table, and peeled off the condom. He wiped himself clean, then crumpled the whole mess together and dropped it onto the floor. "I'll get that later. Don't want to leave the bed now." With another handful of tissues, he dabbed the wetness between her thighs. "Sorry if I got too wild. Did I hurt you?"

Grinning, she shook her head.

He settled onto the pillows, scooped her to his side, and cradled her head on his chest. "In a minute, I'm going to tell you how amazing you are. Rest here with me, okay? You wiped me out." Within two minutes, his breath slowed and deepened into the rhythm of sleep.

She nestled in the inviting hollow below his shoulder and inhaled his scent—fresh sweat and sex musk and lingering notes of citrus shower gel. A wash of tears blurred her vision.

She snuffled and bit her lip. *Just enjoy this for what it is. Don't catch feelings for him.*

But it was too late to guard her heart. Even if it wasn't really love, even if it was only temporary, leaving him behind was going to hurt.

She rested her palm over his steady heartbeat and resolved not to think about the inevitable end. Nestled in the arms of her sweet summer lover, she drifted off to sleep.

# Chapter Eight

♥

The bed creaked and dipped. Danielle's lids fluttered open in time to see Matteo pull his jeans up over his beautiful, taut ass. Standing at the window, he scrubbed his fingers through his sex-tousled hair. His broad, bare shoulders rose and fell on a windy sigh.

Her sweet, sated haze evaporated. He got what he wanted, and now he was leaving. She hugged his discarded pillow to her chest. It still held his scent, his warmth. Tears prickled her eyes. At least she'd have a beautiful memory.

He turned toward her, and a slow-blooming grin spread over his face. "Hey, sorry to wake you." He sat beside her and stroked her bare arm. "I have to go help Zio Sal for a while. Rosa, one of our summer hires, went home sick."

True? False? Did it matter? She released the pillow and entwined her fingers with his. "Sure. Family comes first." Which was exactly why this rosy little romance couldn't last—her kids needed her. She swallowed her disappointment and pasted on what she hoped passed for a smile. "Is Rosa one of your Italian cousins?"

He chuckled. "Just a kid from Sal's church choir. Loves him like a grandpa."

"Ah." She curled her body around his as much as the rumpled covers allowed. "Bet she has a crush on you."

His laughter deepened. "I'm not her favorite flavor. Our Rosa prefers the ladies."

She bit back a totally inappropriate grin.

He wound a tendril of her hair around his forefinger. "So, here's the bad news."

Her stomach muscles clamped down tight as she braced herself for the inevitable kiss-off.

"My friends are getting married on Saturday, one of those hippie beach weddings, and I promised to build them an arch. I'm not even close to done." He leaned onto his elbow and pinned her with a soft gaze. "I want to spend every minute I can with you, but I can't let them down, you know?"

Truth or excuse? She forced herself to breathe evenly.

He smooched her forehead. "Will you be my plus one?"

Dumbfounded, she blinked rapidly. "I—uh—wow."

His bronzed brow rumpled. "Is that too much? Too fast?" He pressed her palm over his heart, and the corner of his mouth twitched upward. "How about if I promise not to propose?"

A laugh spluttered past her tightly clamped lips.

"Tell you what—I won't even catch the bouquet."

Tension unhooked its claws. Giggling, she flopped back onto the pillows. "Okay. Sure. I'd love to come. And I could help you with the arch." She flexed her biceps. "I'm no carpenter, but I've conquered many an Ikea bookshelf."

"Gorgeous and good with an Allen wrench? You are a goddess." He smooched her forehead and bounced up from the bed. "Now where'd my shirt go?"

"Bathroom."

"Right." He flashed a sexy smirk. "How could I forget?" He kissed her hand with so much ardor she very nearly pulled him back into bed. "I never will forget, bella."

His damn phone pinged. "But now, I must go. Call you when I'm done? Maybe if you're not too sore..." He backed from the room, waggling his eyebrows.

"Maybe," she called.

A moment later, the front door closed with a soft click.

Grinning and giddy, she burrowed beneath the covers. "Holy shit. I'm having a fling. I'm a freakin' cougar. The book club would be so proud."

She reached toward the nightstand for her phone but paused, hand in the air. To tell, or not to tell? Their approval would be a welcome balm to her bruised ego. Besides, they were her best friends.

Then again, they'd want to dissect her feelings, and right now, her emotions were a buzzing, sparking tangle. Hell, the whole thing might fizzle out in a few days. Sure, he said he'd call, but perhaps that was the only polite thing to say to a woman whose bones you've just bounced. If they made it to the weekend, she'd tell her friends—after the wedding.

It had been so damn long since she'd had any secrets. Maybe it was selfish, but it was thrilling to have something all her own unconnected to her kids, her job, even her friends.

The phone pinged. On the screen, a photo of a roller-coaster with an insanely steep plunge. Noah wrote,

**Dad totally puked!**

Another photo, her kids grinning between two smirking teen boys. Behind them, Jason looked pale, and Sharla, the girlfriend du jour, looked peeved.

She chuckled. Trouble in paradise?

Funny—in a way, she'd just ridden a roller-coaster of her own.

After a short nap, she rolled out of bed, showered, made a mug of tea, grabbed a paperback, and settled on the deck. The golden sunlight cast long shadows by the time she finished her tea. When she went inside for a refill, she checked her phone. Another photo from Olivia: Noah holding a paper boat of fries. Behind him, Sharla's boys stuck out their tongues and flipped the bird at the camera. Charming.

She composed a message to Jason reminding him to pay attention to the company his kids were keeping, then drew a deep breath and deleted it. Jerk though he may be, he was also a high school principal and knew how to deal with unruly teens.

Her phone lit up with a new photo that sent her pulse into a happy little mambo: Matteo's gorgeous smile above a ridiculously large sundae.

**Not as sweet as you, bella**

She had at least an hour to kill before he closed up shop. Should she walk into town? She glanced over at the fireplace, where her new guitar leaned in its case. What the hell—she had this beautiful place all to herself, with no one to pass judgment on her very rusty playing.

She clipped her nails short on her left hand before carrying the guitar out to the deck, where she lit the gas firepit and settled cross-legged on the chaise lounge. At first, her fingers felt clumsy, but soon muscle memory kicked in, and she strummed the old familiar chords to "Brown-Eyed Girl." Jason used to serenade her with that song, one of the most romantic things he ever did, even though he was mostly tone deaf.

Now it was up to her to sing her own love songs. She kept her voice low at first. Passers-by heading for the beach with their hoodies, folding chairs, and coolers paid her no mind. Caught up in the joy of playing, she sang louder.

Someone joined in. Her head snapped up.

Arms around each other's shoulders, four young women on the corner added their "Sha la la" to the chorus. When the song ended, they clapped and whistled.

Flushed but grinning, she waved. "Thanks. I'll be here all week."

"Put out a tip jar next time," one called as they moved off toward the beach.

She raked a hand through her hair and grinned.

*Guess I've still got it.*

A few hours later, hands aching from the unaccustomed exertion, she laid the guitar aside and rolled her stiff shoulders. Too many years since she'd played this sweet nineties love ballad, and she kept flubbing the lyrics.

"Don't stop. I want to hear the rest of the song."

The firepit's glow didn't extend much past the deck. She peered into the near darkness but couldn't quite make out his face. No mistaking that dark-chocolate voice, though. "Matteo?"

He ambled into view and leaned on the fence, his eyes sparkling in the firelight. "You didn't answer my texts, so I thought I'd cruise by. Hope that's okay."

"Crap. I left my phone inside. Guess I lost track of time."

He hovered at the gate, eyebrows raised.

Uncertain. Just like her.

She beckoned. "I'm glad you came. Join me? I'll put this away."

"Don't." He climbed the steps, sat on the foot of the chaise lounge, and traced the curve of the guitar's body with his fingertip. "You have a beautiful voice, Danielle. I didn't know you played."

She chuckled. "I haven't for years."

"Why not?"

Damn good question. The past few hours had flown by. No intruding thoughts about the divorce, no worries about her kids. She'd fallen into a habit of permanent business, her mind always racing ahead to the next job to be done, the next deadline to hit. But tonight, beneath the velvety summer twilight, she was finally catching her breath—a luxury she wouldn't have for long.

She cleared her throat. "Mom stuff. Work stuff. You know—life."

"The rat race." He slid closer, his thigh against hers. "Don't let it suck all the juice out of your life, bella. I've seen it happen."

"To you?"

He shook his head. "My dad. When I was little, he used to sing to me. Prettiest tenor voice you've ever heard. And when he harmonized with Zio Sal—amazing." Hands clasped, he gazed into the fire. "But he let that damn car dealership swallow up his life. Forgot about music. Said he'd take it up again someday. Then he died."

She gripped his knee. "That's terrible."

Gaze lowered, he nodded. "Tried to pull me down with him." He swiped his eyes with his sleeve, but his voice rang flat, not wobbly with sorrow. "I was supposed to study business, take over the dealership when he retired."

"Not the path for you?"

"Got through two years at U Dub before I dropped out to make furniture." He huffed a bitter laugh. "Dad said I'd never be able to support a family doing that. But what's the point of supporting a family if you never see them?"

She winced as if he'd slapped her.

His hand closed over hers. "Hey, sorry. That was stupid of me. You must miss your kids."

"Yeah, I do. A lot. We've been renting this same house for ten years. I keep hearing their laughter, expecting to see them turn a corner and—I dunno, ask me for ice cream." Her own laugh sounded hollow. "Never enough ice cream. Bottomless stomachs, those two."

He interlaced their fingers. "This must be so hard. But you'll come back here with your kids. Maybe later this summer?"

His expression was so hopeful, she simply had to lean over and kiss him. But introducing the kids to Matteo? She and Jason had forced enough change into their lives already. She couldn't put them through another breakup.

He nudged her shoulder. "You got pictures of them?"

"Sure. And wine. Maybe some food too." She inclined her head toward the house. "You want?"

His chuckle ended on a groan. "Baby, if you're near, I want. And yeah, I could eat."

They assembled a quick picnic of crusty bread, salami, cheese, olives, and strawberries. Matteo carried it out on a tray to enjoy by the fire. Danielle brought quilts from the empty bedrooms, along with wine and glasses. While he uncorked the wine, she pulled up photos of her kids.

"This is Olivia. She's thirteen." Her mud-and-grass-smeared daughter posed with one cleated foot atop a soccer ball, a triumphant grin on her face. "Says she's going to be the next Megan Rapinoe."

He handed her a glass. "Gorgeous, like her mama. What's her position?"

"Forward, but she's hoping to make goalie." She sipped. "And here's Noah." In another post-game photo, her youngest leaned on his lacrosse stick, helmet at his feet, his fair hair mashed and sweaty. His familiar grin tugged hard on her gut. *Miss you, golden boy.*

She forced a steady tone. "Blond, like his dad."

Matteo nodded. "But smarter, I hope."

"What do you mean?"

He slid his arm around her waist. "Any man who would leave you is a Class A idiot. You're so..." He nuzzled her hair. "Warm. Kind. Easy to talk to. Not to mention gorgeous and smart and so sexy you make my insides light up like fireflies."

She leaned into his embrace. "You're sweet, Matteo. But Jason's not stupid so much as restless. And I played my part in our divorce too."

"Well, I guess there's always two sides." He rested his cheek against her hair.

Would Jason have strayed in the first place if she'd been the woman Matteo thought she was? His job placed a lot of demands on him, leaving her to manage the kids' schedules and all the daily crises that came with being a working parent. The last few years, she and Jason spent so little time together, the connection they once shared became thinner and more brittle, until it finally snapped.

In the back of her brain, she heard her book club friends exclaiming that nothing she did would've changed his lying, cheating, scumbag ways. But deep down, she had to wonder.

She nuzzled Matteo's shoulder. "I'm still figuring it all out, and that'll take a while. Which is why you came along at exactly the wrong time."

She stilled, waiting for him to stiffen, to argue, but he just held her quietly. The gas fire flickered and danced. Overhead, a seagull cried. Another answered.

Finally, he squeezed her hand. "You want me to go?"

She closed her eyes and listened hard to her inner voice, the one she usually drowned out with dutiful busyness. She laced her fingers through his.

"No. I want you to stay."

# Chapter Nine

♥

The scent of coffee teased her awake. She yawned and rolled toward the other side of the bed—still warm, but empty. On the pillow, a note:

*Danielle,*

*I don't have words beautiful enough to thank you for last night. Here goes, anyway. Meeting you has been the most wonderful surprise. I must've done something really good in a past life to deserve this.*

*I have to take Sal into Westport for an appointment, then pick up stuff for the wedding arch. We close the gelato shop at seven. Stop by my workshop after? Blue house, right behind Saint Sebastian's. Text me if you can come. Or if you can't. I'll miss you till then.*

*Yours, M*

She pressed the letter over her heart and then, because no one was there to see what a total lovesick sap she'd become, kissed his swooping cursive M.

*Mine—for now.* She counted on her fingers. Eleven more days to enjoy this scary-strong connection. A week from Saturday, she'd be out of this house and on her way back to Tacoma, to her kids and her real life. The thought settled over her like a damp, moldy blanket.

After moping for another fifteen minutes, she rolled to her feet and gave herself a head-to-toe, wet-dog shake. "Enough feeling sorry for myself," she told her nude reflection. "I've got a whole, glorious day at the beach, and I'm probably gonna get lucky tonight."

Even with a sheet-creased face and bed-rumpled hair, she did look pretty good for a middle-aged mom. Glowing, pink, well-rested and well-fucked. Better by far than any spa.

She pulled on yoga pants and an ancient concert T-shirt, then padded barefoot to the kitchen. Sudden tears prickled her eyes when she saw what Matteo had left on the table. A breadbasket held sliced peasant bread, and a bowl of cut melon and strawberries sat beside a plate of cheese, salami, and ham. He'd even set out the butter to soften. A crystal bud vase held a fat ruby geranium from the window box.

What a sweet, thoughtful guy. She removed her phone from the charger, pulled up a playlist of meditation music, and sat down to feast. Afterward, she carried the music into the bathroom and treated herself to a rose-scented bath to soothe her slightly bruised lady parts, lazily reading a paperback mystery until the water cooled. Just for fun, she snapped a selfie of her open book and her wet, bubbly toes beyond, then sent it to her book club group chat.

**Me time**

Proof to Cari, Laurie, and Marie that she was honoring her promise to enjoy her solo vacation. The best part would remain her secret for now.

With a naughty grin, she toweled off, dressed, and arranged her hair on top of her head in a messy bun. Normally, she wore it in a ponytail—but this was a time for trying new styles, new hobbies, even a new persona.

"Why, hello there," she purred into the mirror as she dressed. "I'm Danielle, singer-songwriter and international woman of mystery." With a flip of her full skirt, she stepped out into the glorious sunshine.

All day, she sent her friends and kids a steady stream of photos: the dunes, the beach, Main Street, her new glitter-dusted pedicure, her giant Greek salad with grilled shrimp. She already had hundreds of shots of Trappers Cove, but they centered on her kids doing kid things: collecting seashells, slurping slushies, playing Skee ball in the arcade, driving bumper cars. Though she missed Olivia and Noah fiercely, it was fun examining this well-loved place through a different lens.

On a tip from one of the art gallery owners, she stopped in the town's library to admire its ocean-themed mosaics. Behind the desk, a familiar face smiled. "Hello there. Matteo's friend, right?"

She returned the librarian's smile. "That's me." She extended her hand. "Danielle."

"Right, the speech therapist."

"Um, how—"

The woman patted her hand. "It's a small town, honey. Seems you've made quite an impression on our Italian stallion."

Danielle attempted a carefree laugh, but it came out brittle. "He's a special guy. I'm sure he has lots of women friends."

The librarian shrugged. "Not that I've seen. So, you been to my wife's place yet?"

"I'm not sure. Which shop is hers?"

She tilted her chin. "End of the block. Crystals, fairies, tarot cards. Check it out—she spent all spring sprucing the place up for summer visitors."

"I will, thanks."

Back on the sidewalk, Danielle fanned herself. She'd wanted a glimpse at the real town, but she hadn't counted on being their entertainment.

The tourist crowds were thinner here at the far end of Main Street, where real estate offices mingled with shabby antique shops. The sea breeze lifted Danielle's hair and wafted the scent of sandalwood incense. She followed her nose to a brick-fronted shop, its window filled with tie-dyed T-shirts, crystal skulls, tribal-style jewelry, and a dozen creepy-looking daggers. A carved wooden sign hung above the door: *Madame Zelda's Psychic Emporium*. The curtain of glass beads covering the doorway clicked like chattering teeth as she pushed through.

A few visitors browsed shelves of figurines and racks of jewelry and books. Behind the counter, a plump, petite woman beamed. "Ah, Matteo's sweetheart. I had a hunch you'd stop by. Come, have some tea." She bustled over to a tall wooden cabinet, a wonder of carved embellishments, nooks, shelves, and drawers. Its marble counter held a samovar and chipped China cups. She patted the wood. "Recognize your boyfriend's work?"

Did the whole town know they were together? She accepted a steaming cup of tea that smelled of cardamom and cloves. "Are you Madame Zora?"

The little woman patted her poufy cloud of salt-and-pepper hair. "In the flesh. How about a reading, dear?"

"Oh, I, uh—" No one had read her tarot cards since her woo-woo college roommate.

"On the house, of course." Zora added. "Besides, I'm dying to know about this mystery woman who captured our Matteo's heart."

Embarrassment prickled like sand in her undies. What had Matteo told his neighbors?

"Don't worry, hon. Matteo's not a gossip." The fortuneteller nudged her with a sharp little elbow. "But Mo, the kebab guy, is. We play poker on Tuesdays. Seems our Italian stallion bought a kebab feast for a romantic rendezvous."

She sat at a low table and patted the armchair beside her. "Let's see what the cards say." From a drawer beneath the table, she pulled a deck of tarot cards swathed in red silk, unwrapped them, and handed the deck to Danielle. "While you shuffle, focus on a general area—relationships, health, money, or spiritual growth."

The memory of Matteo's sexy grin tugged her lips into a smile. "Let's do relationships."

While Danielle shuffled the slippery cards, Zora closed her eyes and breathed deeply.

She handed the cards over, and Zora divided them into three piles face down. "Just a simple past, present, future spread." She turned over the top card on the first pile—a prone figure with swords bristling from his back.

Zora winced. "Ten of Swords. Betrayal. End of a relationship. Does this look like your past, hon?"

Danielle gave a dry chuckle. "Yeah, there's definitely a backstabber in my past." Who could blame her for imagining her ex face-down and stuck with swords?

The second card was upside down, a hand holding a five-pointed star encased in a circle. Zora pursed her lips. "Very interesting. Ace of pentacles. A good sign, and a warning."

Danielle's pulse kicked up a notch. "Warning about what?"

"Well, in relationships, it means you risk missing out on love." She tapped the previous card. "Most likely, this experience left you feeling vulnerable, out of balance. Don't rush getting to know this new person. True connection needs time and attention to grow."

Danielle bit her lip. Zora must be in league with the matchmaking nonnas.

"Ready for the last card? Your future?"

Still nibbling her lip, she nodded. The third card featured a robed angel pouring water from one chalice to another.

Zora beamed. "Ah, this is a good one. Temperance. Sign of healing, of combining different elements to make something better."

Danielle gulped and stared into the fortuneteller's eyes—kind eyes, crinkled at the corners, sharp and knowing. A funny, fizzy sensation filled her chest. Must be all the onions on that Greek salad.

Chuckling, Zora wrapped her Tarot deck and placed it back in the drawer. "A skeptic would say that's generic advice, right?" She leaned forward. "Doesn't make it any less effective, though."

Danielle nodded, squirming in her chair. Despite the mellow music floating from the speakers and the soft murmurs of customers, something about the dark little shop made her itchy to escape. Perhaps it was the figurines staring at her from the shelves: Buddhas, Ganeshas, Mexican sugar skulls, mischievous fairies, brooding wizards, snarling dragons...

She gave her head a little shake and drained her cup. "Well, thanks for the tea. And the wisdom."

"My pleasure, dear. Come back if you have any questions. Or just to browse our crystals." Zora swept a hand toward the glass counter where colorful stones rested in velvet-lined trays. "Chrysocolla is good for feminine wisdom and balance. Also good for musicians like you."

Danielle spluttered. "How did you—?"

"Your nails are shorter on your left hand." The older woman grinned. "Besides, I do yoga with Annie from the antiques shop."

Danielle backed toward the door. "Guess I can't expect to keep secrets in a small town."

The soothsayer lifted a single brow. "No indeed. But in exchange for your privacy, you could gain a lot of love."

# Chapter Ten

❤

Four hours later, Danielle pulled up to a ramshackle Craftsman cottage the color of a motel swimming pool. An eclectic collection of beachy knickknacks lined the porch railing: starfish, hurricane lamps, fishing nets, glass floats, and painted terracotta mermaids. A wooden staircase led to an apartment above the detached two-car garage.

Blues music drifted through the open garage door, interrupted by the shriek of a power tool. The thought of Matteo's hands mastering powerful machines set off a giddy tingle low in her belly.

In her rearview mirror, she straightened the silk scarf she'd folded into a headband, slicked on more lipstick, then blotted it. *Stop dithering!* She'd already had mind-blowing sex with Matteo, already spent a whole night wrapped in his arms. But after the fortuneteller's predictions, she couldn't shake the feeling there was more at stake here than a mere fling.

Eleven more days. Ridiculous, thinking they could last beyond that deadline. If she had the common sense God gave a goose, she'd throw her car into reverse and forget this vacation romance nonsense.

Matteo stepped into the open doorway, holding a power drill at his hip like some rumpled sci-fi hero gripping his ray gun—an impression that strengthened when he abled toward her, flashing that seductive smile of his. A worn concert T-shirt stretched tight across his broad chest, and paint-stained jeans clung to his muscular thighs. She forced her gaze up from the enticing bulge below his belt, back up to his dazzling smile. Pale flakes dusted the sexy scruff on his jaw. Sawdust? Might as well be stardust because she was powerless to look away.

He leaned an elbow on the roof of her car and grinned through the open window. "Ciao, bella. I'm glad you came."

She boosted up to kiss him and darted her tongue into the silky heat of his mouth. His fingers tightened on the drill, making it whir.

"Careful, now." Laughing, he opened her door. "High-voltage kisses and power tools—not a good combination." He slung his free arm around her shoulders and walked her back to the garage. She squeezed his waist, and the drill whirred again.

"You're dangerous, Danielle." He set the drill on a crowded workbench, pulled a bandana from his pocket, and dusted off a metal stool. "Your throne, my queen. Welcome to my atelier. Also known as Sal's garage."

Filling one wall, sturdy metal shelves held tools, brushes, cans of paint and varnish, plus trays of drawer pulls, handles, and other hardware. Shelves along the other wall held table legs, boards, and window frames. Photos and sketches hung from a corkboard on the rear wall. In the center of the room sat a rusted garden arbor half-covered with driftwood.

Matteo pointed to the ceiling. "I live upstairs."

"You don't share the house with Sal?"

"We tried that, but he's an early riser. Likes to practice opera while he makes breakfast. First time he blasted Nessun Dorma at six a.m., I nearly pissed myself."

She giggled at the image of a sleep-rumpled Matteo bolting out of bed. She'd much rather see him waking gently beside her, his warm, sleepy-soft body spooned against hers...

She cleared her throat and forced her attention back to the present moment. "Have you lived here long?"

"Since November. Sal needed help when Zia Giulia got sick." He stared into the distance, his gaze misty. "Breast cancer. Took her so damn fast. I lost my job in Seattle, and Sal offered me this place. Kind of a lifesaver for me."

"I'll bet you're a big help to him too."

He shrugged. "I try to be useful. He could barely manage the shop without Giulia's help. What they had was really special." He smiled and clasped her hand, his thumb tracing arcs over her knuckles. "Anyway, I picked up the slack at the gelato shop. I'm happy here." He rolled up an extension cord snaking across the floor. "Sal and me, we're simpatico, you know? Refugees from the rat race. He sings his opera, I make my furniture, and we both sling gelato." He clapped his hands and rubbed them together. "So, you hungry? Sal's fixing dinner for us."

She chuckled. "Seems you're always feeding me, Matteo. You should let me cook for you."

He waved away her protest with a flick of his fingers. "You're on vacation. You don't have to be the mom all the time."

That reminder poked like a rusty pin. Olivia and Noah had sent dozens of photos throughout the day—on midway rides, eating great piles of junk food, and mugging with the girlfriend's sons. Years of working with kids had sharpened her radar, and those boys beamed an up-to-no-good vibe. Not much she could do about it, though.

She cleared her throat. "I like to cook. Besides, I have that big kitchen to myself."

He pulled her to her feet, slid his hands around her hips, and nuzzled the sensitive crook of her neck. "It's a date, then, as soon as I finish this project. You cook, and I'll do the dishes." The way he nibbled her earlobe, "doing the dishes" must be code for something dirty and delicious.

Sal banged on the rear window with his fist and called, "Mangiamo."

Matteo tugged her toward the door. "You mind sharing dinner with Sal?"

"Of course not. He's my second-favorite Italian."

Matteo switched off the music and lights, then led her to a patio of flagstones interspersed with colorful bits of broken tile. Fairy lights twinkled overhead, suspended from posts at the corners. Against the garden wall, a lopsided Venus poured water into a giant cement clamshell. The merry trickle complemented the chatter of swallows swooping low over the grass.

Dapper in a white dress shirt, slacks, and striped suspenders, Sal unloaded dishes from a tray. He glanced up and flashed a broad grin. "Buona sera, Danielle. So glad you could join us."

Her mouth watered as Sal arranged a cold supper of marinated grilled vegetables, crusty bread, salad, and a platter of thin-sliced meat covered with a pale, creamy sauce. She pointed. "Is that—"

"Vitello tonnato," he replied with a flourish, then winked. "Actually, it's roast turkey. Wasn't sure if you eat veal. Lots of people don't, these days."

Matteo whistled. "Sal, you said you were just making sandwiches and salad."

"Bah." Sal waved dismissively. "Fran owed me a favor, since I sang at her granddaughter's wedding." He pulled out a seat for Danielle. "You know Casa Francesca? Best pasta alle vongole on the Washington coast. Next time, we'll go with your kids. They'll love Fran's lasagna." He kissed his fingertips.

The mention of her kids zinged her with guilt, which was ridiculous. They were having a blast in SoCal. She wasn't harming them by having dinner with her new friends. And unlike Jason, she had no intention of introducing them to

Matteo. Unless... The fortuneteller's voice echoed: *Combining different elements to make something better.*

She unfurled her linen napkin and waved away those nagging thoughts.

Sal shooed Matteo. "Go clean up, boy. You dishonor Fran's fine cooking."

Matteo gave a staccato bow and dashed up the stairs to his apartment. Sal uncorked the wine.

"Pinot Grigio. From the Willamette Valley, not Italy, but it's pretty good." He poured a generous glassful and slid it toward her.

She sipped tart, bright sunshine. "Delicious."

Sal filled his own glass and sat beside her. "So, bella, have you found what you're looking for?"She blinked rapidly. "Sorry?"

His warm, calloused hand covered hers. "You could have spent your vacation with friends, but you came here. Alone. When a person does that, she is searching for something. Maybe out in the world, maybe in here." He tapped his sternum.

She dropped her gaze to their joined hands. Here was a man who'd lost his great love but seemed happy. She'd lost her—well, perhaps it had never been more than a mediocre love. Her drive to be the perfect mom and speech therapist left her with too little time, too little focus to nourish their marriage. Not that she blamed herself for Jason's cheating ways. She'd been unfulfilled too, but she'd never broken her marriage vows. Still, there was something he needed that he didn't get from her.

Sal squeezed her hand. "I'm glad to see Matteo keeping company with someone like you. A lady of substance."

She glanced down at her wide lap.

"No, no, no, bella. I'm not talking about your figure. Which is perfect, by the way. A woman should have curves, in my opinion." He tapped his forehead. "I mean, you got smarts.

And heart. Your idiot husband screwed things up, but you didn't crumble. And I'll tell you—" He leaned onto his elbow and lowered his voice. "My Matteo, he's got heart, too. A huge one. Smart, handsome kid like him coulda found another job in Seattle like that." He snapped his fingers. "But he came here to help his old uncle. He puts people first, you know?"

So did she. The trouble was, her kids had to come before all the other people in her life. Herself included.

For a long moment, they sat in silence, watching the swallows' acrobatics in the gathering dusk. Sal's cozy little yard was a good place to sit with her thoughts and feelings—just breathe it all in, along with the scent of summer green and salty ocean.

Upstairs, a door slammed. Sal chuckled. "My nephew's making himself pretty for you." He stabbed an olive, then wagged his fork. "I'll give you a little free wisdom before dinner. Take it or leave it."

She nodded. Without Sal's invitation to the Sons of Italy banquet, she probably would have spent her vacation holed up with paperbacks and boxed wine. If he wanted to pontificate, she'd gladly listen.

He popped the olive into his mouth, chewed thoughtfully for a long moment, then pointed again with his fork. "Life's too short." His warm chestnut eyes lasered into hers. "You know what I mean?"

"Too short for what?"

His lips hitched in a melancholy smile. "Just too short. Don't waste it. If you love something, make time for it."

"If you love someone, you mean?"

He shrugged. "A person, a place, a hobby, a passion. Whatever you love, fill your life with that. Because life's too damn short." He dabbed his lips with his napkin, then blotted his eyes. Her heart squeezed.

Matteo thundered down the stairs and trotted to Sal's side, smelling of soap and sandalwood. He'd traded his stained work clothes for a dark blue dress shirt, ivory linen pants, and leather flip flops. He spread his arms and rotated in a slow circle. "Okay, Zio. Am I worthy of Fran's cooking?"

"Much better." Sal leaned onto his elbow and hooked a thumb over his shoulder. "Che bel ragazzo, eh? What a handsome guy."

She grinned. "Like his uncle."

They dug into their feast. The creamy, subtle tonnato sauce, studded with briny capers, was the perfect foil for the tender braised turkey breast. Manners be damned. She mopped up the last bit of sauce with her bread. While they ate, Sal regaled them with stories about their family—Matteo's snarky, artistic sister who lived in Portland with her girlfriend, also his mom, who'd found love with—gasp!—a non-Italian and moved to California. "Only six months after her husband died. Che scandalo." Sal scooped more salad onto her plate. "But I say—well, you know my position." He winked.

Matteo shrugged. "LeVon's a good guy. He treats her well. She deserves to be happy."

Sal pushed back from the table. "I'll clean up. You youngsters stay and talk." He inclined his head toward a small balcony above the patio. "Nice view up there. You can see the dunes."

Matteo rose and extended his hand. "What do you say, bella? We're trying a new gelato flavor, salted caramel with hazelnuts. Got some in my freezer."

She didn't bother hiding her wide smile. *Pretty sure we're going to share something much tastier than gelato.*

# Chapter Eleven

♥

Holding her hand, Matteo led her up the stairs. "Sorry about Sal. He's as bad a matchmaker as the nonnas. Shoulda told him about my promise not to pressure you."

Matteo was right, but she couldn't resent the old guy for his loving intentions. "He means well. He loves you and wants you to be happy."

Clasping her hips, he danced her through the doorway. "You know, I'm pretty damn happy at the moment."

Danielle kicked off her sandals beside the front door and surveyed Matteo's home. Though small, the apartment felt airy and open. An eclectic mix of paintings, posters, and photos covered the walls. A squashy leather loveseat and chairs clustered around a colorful Kilim rug, facing one of those ski-chalet mini fireplaces. The sitting area, dining table, and kitchenette took up two-thirds of the space, separated from the bedroom by a divider of wooden crates holding vases, bowls, and other artsy knickknacks. She stroked the glossy wood. "Clever. Your work?"

"Yeah. Got a good deal on crates from a defunct cannery. Amazing what you can build with these. End tables, desks, platform beds, you name it." He switched on a small speaker, and soft jazz filled the apartment. He stepped up behind her and trailed his fingertips down her ribs to the swell of her hips.

"Didn't have much time to clean up, so don't peek under the furniture."

Sighing, she leaned back into his embrace. "I don't care if you have dust bunnies the size of Texas." *Do you have any idea how amazing you are?* she added silently.

He planted a soft kiss on her temple, then moved to the kitchen where he scooped gelato into earthenware bowls. "Shall we eat this outside? We can watch the sunset."

She followed him through French doors onto a balcony just big enough for two rattan chairs and a small table. He lit a pair of hanging lanterns suspended from the latticework roof. Golden flame danced behind frosted glass inscribed with stars and moons. Below, the fountain burbled, and a rising breeze stirred wind chimes suspended from trees below, a tinkling farewell to the sun's last rays. Over the rooftops and sinuous curves of the dunes, the horizon bloomed a vibrant fuchsia that faded to orange, then indigo.

So different from her yard in Tacoma, with its giant trampoline and patchy lawn that demanded constant mowing. How sweet it would be to sit here with Matteo, watching the sunsets change as summer rolled into golden autumn, followed by stormy winter.

Right. And the kids would be where, exactly? Playing video games on his TV?

She tried a spoonful of creamy, sweet-salty gelato. "So good," she moaned.

Matteo watched her, a cryptic half-smile on his face. He took a bite and licked his spoon clean.

Low in her belly, a swarm of fireflies ignited.

He inclined his head toward the interior. "I worried about asking you up. Not a very impressive apartment."

"Well, I'm glad you did. And I like your place. It's artistic. Comfortable. Surprising. Like you."

He flashed an adorable aw-shucks grin and dug into his dessert.

She snuck glances between bites, mesmerized by the slow, sensuous movement of his lips and tongue over the spoon. Finally, he pushed his empty bowl away. "Should have asked you to bring your guitar. I'd love to hear you sing again."

"Pssshh." She swatted away his compliment. "I'm an off-key amateur. It'll take me months to get my chops back. Maybe years."

Maybe never. You can't turn the clock back.

"Bullshit, bella," he countered. "You have a beautiful voice. Rich and round, like a good Chianti. And you play that guitar like it's part of your body."

She rolled her eyes, sure he was just trying to get her back into his bed—not that she needed much persuasion.

Reaching across the table, he took her hand. "Everyone needs a creative outlet. Otherwise, your soul shrivels up like a prune. Saw that happen to my dad. He let that damn car dealership suck all the joy out of his life." He pulled her to her feet and wrapped his arms loosely around her waist. The candlelight flickered and danced in his espresso-dark eyes. "Don't let that happen to you. Stay juicy, bella."

There was no denying how juicy she felt in his arms. Whether that had to do with his creativity, or hers, was an open question. But being with him sparked visions of how much fulfilling her life could be—someday, when the kids were older. When they didn't need her to be their taxi driver, academic coach, and all-around support team.

Reality rolled in like fog, damp and cold. "Eleven more days," she muttered.

"Is that truly all you want?" He pressed his lips behind her ear, and the fireflies in her belly became fireworks. "Think about it, Danielle. Our connection is amazing. I'm not sure why that is—chemistry, destiny, or just dumb luck—but we deserve more than eleven days." He lifted her hair and trailed kisses down the back of her neck.

Drawn by the light, a moth bopped against her cheek. With a deep, sexy laugh, Matteo released her and opened the French doors. "Inside? Fewer bugs."

Sexy saxophone music sighed and moaned from the speaker on the counter. Taking her hand, he led her to a clear spot beside the front door. "Dance with me, bella?"

He could have pulled her straight to his bed. Already, she was flushed and slick with desire, but Matteo was in no hurry. He made it so easy to relax in his arms and sway to the music's lazy beat. So easy to forget the world outside this cozy nest. Just two bodies moving to the same rhythm, two hearts beating in time.

Her fingertips toyed with the open collar of his shirt. Satin skin, soft hair, strong pulse. She pressed a kiss to the notch in his collar bone.

Spearing his fingers into her hair, he angled her head back and pressed his mouth to hers. His tongue teased her lips apart, then swept inside, all velvet sweetness and slow, sure strokes.

There was magic in his kiss, a sensual balm that quieted her doubts and gave her the rare gift of savoring the moment. Didn't matter if he embraced her on the dance floor, on the beach, in her cottage, or here in his cozy apartment, Matteo's succulent kisses anchored her to the present. She angled her head to welcome his unhurried exploration.

He pressed her against the cool wood of the front door, cupped her face in both hands, and fixed her with a glittering dark gaze. "Beautiful Danielle, you are..." He sighed and touched his forehead to hers. "A class act. Kind, funny, smart. What are you doing with a beach bum like me?" He unknotted the silk scarf holding her hair, wove his fingers into her curls, and trailed hot, wet kisses down her throat.

What was a gorgeous young artist like Matteo doing with a suburban drudge like her?

She raked her fingers through his soft mane. "I'm having more fun than I've had in years. Too many years." It was easy to tell him the truth, since he'd be gone from her life soon. "You're a treasure, Matteo. I wish I could keep you, but I can't. So let's enjoy today."

"You deserve to enjoy every day, bella. Don't forget that." With a sexy animal grunt, he sank to his knees, raised her skirt, and whispered kisses over her inner thighs. Her core clenched and throbbed, craving his touch. He slid her panties down, lifted her leg onto his shoulder, and with a soft exclamation, buried his face between her thighs.

All thoughts of tomorrow drowned in a wave of pleasure as his tongue performed its magic. Long, lingering strokes, feathery licks, gentle nibbles, and firm suction on her clit that pulled her right to the edge of bliss. Too fast. If she only had eleven more days to indulge her sensual whims, she was damn sure going to taste them all. Starting now.

"Stop." She unwound herself from his embrace and pulled him to his feet. "I want my turn."

She tugged her blouse over her head, then unfastened her skirt and let it fall. With a giddy whoop, she flung her bra across the room.

Matteo gaped, chest heaving, his erection tenting his linen pants.

He must be going commando again, naughty boy. She scooped up the silk scarf, wound it around her neck, and stroked the cool fabric over her breasts.

His gaze slid over her naked form as he unbuttoned his shirt.

"No." She spun him so his back rested against the door and pinned his wrists at his sides. "Let me. Keep your hands here."

His eyes widened, and he flattened his palms on the wood.

A heady, almost drunken sensation swam through her veins. Who was this wanton woman? Where had she been hiding all these years? No matter—it was her turn to take control. Licking her lips, she unfastened his shirt buttons.

He gulped, his Adam's apple bobbing, but let her undress him without protest. She kissed each inch of exposed skin and ran greedy palms over the smooth planes of his chest. His belly tensed beneath her hands. When she sank to her knees and hooked her fingertips into his waistband, he clenched his fists.

Barely restrained by the loose linen, his erection jutted up and out. She pressed her lips to the tip and heated the cloth with her breath.

"Bella, please." His breath shuddered as she stroked his length, then unknotted the drawstring at his waist. One quick tug, and his pants fell to the floor.

She sat back on her heels and admired the delectable treat before her, long and thick, its rosy crown weeping a tear of pleasure. "Ciao, bello." Corny, but she couldn't resist. Just to prolong his sweet torture, she stroked his length with her scarf and ran the cool silk over his plump balls. His strangled cry landed somewhere between a groan and a growl.

Encircling his shaft with both hands, she took the plush crown into her mouth. Immediately, his hips began to buck, a small, instinctive movement that made her shiver with need. His fingers threaded into her hair and softly kneaded her scalp, but he let her set the pace, never pushing too hard. She licked him from root to tip, teasing him with nips and nibbles, all the while stroking his balls and cock with her scarf. Such a mesmerizing contrast—silk over hot stone.

Face flushed, eyes hooded, he lolled his head against the door and surrendered to her greedy hands and tongue—until his body jolted. He grasped her shoulders and pulled free from her mouth, panting, "Bella, I want to finish inside you. Please." Feeling every inch the sultry temptress, she draped the damp scarf over her shoulders and flashed a wicked smile as she swirled the silk around one aching nipple.

With a growl, he yanked her to her feet and pressed her against the door. Her scarf slithered to the floor. His erection poked her belly, then slid lower to glide in the slickness of her arousal while he pinched and rolled her nipples. Fierce need flared deep inside. She wrapped one thigh around his waist and angled her hips until his blunt crown notched at her entrance.

He hissed and jerked backward. "Condom."

*Oh my God, we almost*—Chest heaving, she  gulped air while he sheathed himself.

He snatched up her scarf and turned her to face the breakfast bar. His breath hot on her nape, he wound the silk around the kitchen spigot, then around her wrists. Not too tight, just a symbolic binding, but the feeling of yielding control to Matteo fired her blood. She bit her lip and arched her back as he nudged her feet apart. The taut head of his cock prodded her entrance. With a ragged groan, he drove into her in one deep stroke that stole her breath.

He pummeled her, his hips slapping hard and fast against her ass while his cock did magical things inside her. His breath came shallow and ragged, but his nimble fingers slid through her slick arousal and found her clit, circling, circling. She gripped the counter and shoved her hips backward, meeting him thrust for delicious thrust.

"God, Matteo, so good, so good." Her words dissolved into moans.

He slowed his movements to prolong the last delirious moments. She trembled on the edge, barely breathing.

His fingers tightened on her hip, his voice strained. "Now, bella. Come for me now." He pinched her clit and drove his cock in to the root.

With a high, keening cry, she let go. Spirals of impossible pleasure lifted her onto her toes. Matteo clutched her close, his sweaty chest against her back as he shuddered and gasped.

Gradually the sparks winked out, her breath slowed, and her twitching muscles relaxed. Matteo's damp palms stroked her flanks. His breath hot against her ear, he murmured, "Danielle Delfino, you are a goddess."

Her chuckle was threaded with bitterness. "My last name is Peters."

"Bullshit." He gave a final thrust before withdrawing. "That bastard left you. Take your name back, bella. Take your life back." He kissed between her shoulder blades. "Take me with you."

Her spine stiffened. Beautiful words, but what did they really mean?

He unknotted the scarf and eased her onto a stool, then trotted to the bathroom and returned a moment later with a fluffy hand towel and a sheepish expression. Lips pressed together, he watched while she blotted between her legs.

*God, I don't want to tell him, but I have to.* "Matteo—"

"Look, I—" He balled up the towel and held it to his chest. "Bella, I'm sorry. You make me crazy in the best possible way, and I say things I shouldn't. I know you've got a life away from here, your kids, your job, your friends. I respect that. I'm just—" His sculpted shoulders rose and fell. "I wish I could be a part of it."

Her gut vibrated like a plucked guitar string.

She slid her arms around his neck and held him close, rocking slowly to the music—a tenor sax solo, sultry and mournful. "I have to put my kids first." She stroked his back and fought the ache behind her eyes.

This was insane. She wasn't supposed to meet someone like Matteo, and she damn sure wasn't supposed to have feelings for him. He was too young, too far away, too perfect to be real.

He pressed his forehead to hers. "I know. That asshat ripped a hole in your family. You've gotta keep your kids safe." He kissed her brow. "And I'm not asking you to move here. Though I bet your kids would love it."

"Their friends—"

"Yeah, of course. At their age, friends are the most important thing." He stroked his thumbs over her cheekbones. "But you're important too, Danielle. Don't forget that. You deserve happiness." He kissed her. "I'd give anything for the chance to make you happy."

She stroked his cheek. "A wise woman told me only I can do that."

Three wise women, actually: her book club posse. One divorced like her, one fighting to hold her marriage together through the exhausting toddler years, and one never married, though she raised two bright, beautiful daughters. All agreed that no man could truly make a woman happy—she had to do that on her own, with or without a partner. But could Matteo be part of her happiness?

This wasn't fair to him, with her living so far away. Once their two weeks were up and she returned to Tacoma, he'd find a more suitable woman, someone not tied down by young kids and a demanding job. Someone creative and flexible, who'd fit into this funky little apartment—who'd fit into his carefree life.

Blinking back tears, she buried her face in the crook of his neck and inhaled his scent—warm skin and fresh sweat, sunshine and promises. "Eleven days, Matteo. And then we'll talk."

*And then I'll tell you goodbye.*

# Chapter Twelve

♥

"Freakin' gorgeous!" Danielle set down her hot glue gun and fished in the pocket of the stained coveralls she'd borrowed from Matteo. Her phone was in there somewhere, beneath a crumpled rag and snippets of cloth. She circled the wedding arch and snapped photos from different angles. For the past two days, she'd helped him encase the metal arbor's uprights in driftwood and top them with a wooden arch salvaged from a defunct chapel. This afternoon, while Matteo scooped gelato, she draped the structure with tulle in sea-foam green and sky blue, the couple's favorite colors, and wound the uprights in satin ribbon. Tomorrow, the florist would weave in fresh flowers to complete the perfect backdrop for a beach wedding.

She peeled off the coveralls, then sent the photos to Matteo. His reply came back within seconds.

**It's beautiful, bella! You're so creative.**

Grinning, she removed her bandana and fluffed her squashed hair. Who'da thunk it? The mom who flunked Pinterest had actually mastered a craft project. Brimming with pride, she loaded photos into a group text to her book club friends, but she froze with her finger over the Send button. If she told them, she'd have to explain why she built the thing in the first place. She'd have to explain about Matteo.

She wasn't ready yet. Maybe after the wedding. She sank onto a stool. Maybe not at all.

At first, she'd enjoyed having a secret, something that was hers alone. But over the past week, as her connection with Matteo deepened, she craved the help of her girlfriends to answer the question that followed her all day and woke her in the middle of the night: Could this be something?

She chewed her lip, staring at the phone. It pinged and flashed Olivia's number.

**Mom, call?**

Her belly tightened as she pressed Call Back. Today the kids were at Universal Studios. Had one of them fallen off a ride? Been bitten by a mechanical dinosaur? Gotten sick from too many curly fries?

Olivia's hushed voice was hard to hear over yelling in the background. "Hey, Mom. We've got a problem."

Adrenaline pushed Danielle to her feet. "What's going on? Where are you?"

"In the parking lot. We got kicked out of the park."

"What the—why?"

Noah's gruff voice broke through. Only ten, he sounded more like a teen every day. "Give me the phone." Sounds of arguing, then, "Jayden and Brayden tried to steal magic wands from the wizard shop. This huge security guy caught them. It was scary." But kind of cool, his giddy tone suggested.

Her jaws clenched. "Put your father on the phone."

"But Mom, he—"

"Now, please."

More background hubbub, and finally, Jason's tight voice. "It's under control, Danielle."

"Is it?" she snapped. "Pretty shitty example those boys are setting for our kids."

"I said, I've got it handled. Sharla will discipline her boys. I'll talk with Olivia and Noah."

"And you'll make it clear this bullshit behavior is in no way acceptable or even remotely cool?"

His voice dropped to a growl, a tone she recognized all too well. "I said—"

But she was so over bowing to his moods. "I've gotta wonder how a high school principal failed to notice those boys were trouble. I've gotta wonder about your priorities, Jason, and your judgment." She strangled the phone. "I've gotta wonder if I should interrupt my vacation and come get our kids."

"Your vacation? Where are you?"

"At the beach house, of course, since your last-minute surprise stuck me with the bill."

"You went by yourself?" Why did he sound so incredulous? Did he think she'd just mope around Tacoma for two weeks?

She swiped a hand down her face. Okay, she'd nearly done that, but things had changed. She'd changed.

His voice softened. "Well, good. I'm glad you're able to enjoy it. And I'll deal with this mess. See you on the sixth." Not quite an apology, but further parental warfare would only hurt the kids.

Her mood spoiled, she disconnected the call, heaved a weary sigh, and gathered her things. As she drove back to the rental house, the sunshine reached that glorious, golden, early-evening hue. She had barely enough time to shower and finish dinner, now simmering in a Crockpot. Thank the gods Trappers Cove's little food co-op had all the ingredients: a whole chicken, a good dry red, and fresh herbs. It was her turn to spoil Matteo with a home-cooked meal—and in other, creative ways.

She pulled onto her street and stomped on the brakes. "What the...?"

Someone was lounging on her deck! Three someones, in fact. Cari, Laurie, and Marie popped to their feet and waved, all three wearing neon fabric leis and goofy sunglasses. Paper cups and a half-empty wine bottle sat on the rim of the fire pit.

"Surprise!" They thundered down the steps, arms waving like a middle-aged cheer squad.

Danielle parked in the driveway behind Laurie's SUV. Cari yanked open the door, pulled Danielle to her feet, and enveloped her in a squishy hug.

"I thought you were all tied up this weekend," Danielle squeaked.

Marie popped a lei over Danielle's head. "Our friend needed us. Girls' party weekend!"

"You have this big house to yourself, so we're having a slumber party." Laurie poked neon-pink sunglasses into Danielle's face. "We brought lots of wine and snacks."

"And fancy face masks," Cari added, tugging her up the deck stairs. "Plus a little something special just for you." She winked, and all three giggled.

Marie dug in her enormous purse and handed over a gift-wrapped box. "Open it!"

"No, she needs wine first."

Danielle scrubbed both palms down her face and sank into a chair. "Guys, this is really sweet, but—"

Laurie shoved a brimming cup of rosé into her hand. "Drink up! We're way ahead of you."

*No shit.* Stifling a groan, she gulped her wine, opened the package, and pulled out a purple silicone dildo.

"It's called the Unicorn," Cari explained. "See, it's got separate controls for this part and this part." Leaning over Danielle's shoulder, she pressed a button, and the gizmo buzzed and writhed. All three friends shrieked with laughter.

Laurie clapped her on the shoulder. "Meet your new boyfriend."

*Boyfriend!* Panic seized her, and she fumbled for her phone. She had to warn Matteo.

Cari whistled. "Ooh là là. Who's this?"

She whirled to find him at the gate, clutching a bouquet and a bottle of wine. He shot her a quizzical look, then flashed a dazzling smile, climbed the stairs, and kissed her cheek. "Friends of yours?" he whispered.

She nodded.

"Were you expecting them?" She shook her head.

"Well then." He set down his load and wound his arm around her waist.

She gulped. "Guys, meet Matteo."

For a long, silent moment, the three women goggled at him. Finally, Cari cleared her throat and approached, hand extended. "Pleased to meet you, Matteo." She nudged Danielle with her elbow. "You've been keeping secrets, Dani."

Matteo shook hands with each friend in turn, his wide smile strained and tight.

"Would you excuse us a minute, ladies?" He took her hand and pulled her toward the sidewalk. "You want to scrap tonight?" he asked, his voice low.

"No!" She gripped his forearm. "They were worried about me, all alone in this big house. They came to cheer me up."

"You didn't tell them about us." His eyes narrowed. "You ashamed of me, bella?"

She cupped his jaw in both hands. "No, I swear. I just—wanted more time. Just the two of us, you know? When we're together, I can forget about what came before and what comes next."

He regarded her for a long moment, breathing hard through flared nostrils. Then his eyes closed, and his brow smoothed. "Okay, I promised not to pressure you. But I do think about what comes next, bella. I think about it all the time." The corner of his mouth hitched in a wry smile. "Now, you gonna feed me, or what?"

· ❤ · ❤ · ❤ · ❤ · ❤ ·

Danielle pushed back from the dining table. Thank God she'd bought the biggest chicken in the meat case. Supplemented with roasted potatoes, salad, and lots of bread, her coq au vin stretched to feed five, barely. In the kitchen, Matteo hummed as he washed dishes—the clatter and splash a thoughtful cover for their dissection of his finer points.

"Oh my God, Dani, he's adorable," Marie squeaked and squeezed Danielle's wrist.

Only half-listening to her friends' chatter, Danielle watched him through the open doorway, the smooth shifting of his muscles beneath his chambray shirt, the way his worn jeans cupped his ass.

"...tell your kids?" Laurie asked.

She shook her lust-addled head. "Sorry, what?"

"When will you tell them?"

She reached for a cookie, stalling.

"Dani, you have to tell them."

She dropped her head into her hands. "I know, but I don't want to be like Jason."

Cari snorted. "How could you possibly compare yourself to that schmuck?"

She quickly related that afternoon's phone call. "Three times, now, he's introduced them to his squeeze du jour. They always break up as soon as the kids start to feel comfortable with her. It's not fair to them. They need at least one stable parent."

"So, keeping secrets equals protecting your kids?" Laurie nabbed a cookie with pink icing and sprinkles. "Or are you just protecting yourself?"

Danielle groaned and slumped onto the table. "There's no way this can last. He's so damned young."

Cari snorted. "He doesn't seem to care about your age."

"For now."

Marie snatched the last jam-filled cookie. "Try listening to him instead of listening to your fear. Just because stupid-ass Jason left you doesn't mean every guy's gonna leave you."

The clatter in the kitchen stopped, replaced by approaching footsteps. Danielle bolted upright.

Matteo gently gripped her shoulder. "Well, ladies, I think I'd better leave. It was a pleasure meeting you all. I hope to see you again soon. Bella, will you see me out?"

She followed him to the deck.

He twined a lock of her hair around his finger. "So, did I pass inspection?"

"You got an A-plus." She slid her arms around his neck and kissed him. "Thanks for being so understanding." Another kiss, longer and deeper. "Do you really want to go?"

He chuckled against her temple. "Of course I don't. Only eight more days until you kick me to the curb. But you should spend time with your friends." He flashed a devilish grin and squeezed her ass with both hands. "Maybe they'll talk you into giving me a chance."

She arched an eyebrow. "Maybe they'll talk me out of it."

"It's a calculated risk." He kissed her again, deep and slow and sweet. "I'll pick you up tomorrow at three."

For a moment she blinked up at him, her mind blanked by his kiss, his heat, his delectable, distracting, muscly maleness.

His smile twitched with suppressed laughter. "The wedding?"

"Oh, right. Can't miss that." She gave him a lingering goodnight kiss before reluctantly letting him go.

Back inside, she faced her giddy girlfriends, huddled over the dining table. "So, um..."

They popped to their feet and, squeeing like middle schoolers, trotted over to envelop her in a squishy group hug.

"He is so freakin' cute!"

"I'm so jealous, Dani."

"What's he like in bed?"

Without giving her a chance to answer, they tugged her into the living room, where a pile of shopping bags covered the coffee table. Marie reached into one and pulled out a handful of shiny foil packets. "Okay, first the face masks and chocolate martinis, then we grill Dani about her boy toy."

Cari unpacked the bottles. "And you'd better talk fast, because we're leaving right after breakfast."

Danielle protested, "First, he's not a toy. Second, I thought you were spending the weekend." The three friends exchanged a meaningful look.

"Well, you've got the wedding," Marie started.

"And my sitter has a thing tomorrow," Laurie added.

Cari poured vodka into a cocktail shaker, followed by a slug of cream. "Cut the crap, you guys." She added a generous splash of chocolate liqueur. "Dani, we came to keep you company. But you already have company. And we're proud of you." She shook the mixture with ice and poured it into tumblers. "Here's to you, Dani, and your sweet young thing."

They clinked.

Danielle sipped and winced. "Holy cow, that's strong." She held up her glass for another toast. "Here's to the best friends a girl could have. And I call dibs on the rose petal mask."

# Chapter Thirteen

♥

"I wasn't looking for a new partner." The bride in blue sniffed hard before continuing. "I sure as hell didn't expect to fall in love."

The bride in green stamped her bare foot in the sand and muttered, "Well, shit. So much for getting through this without crying."

Laughing along with the other wedding guests, Danielle dabbed her tears and glanced at Matteo, whose eyes shone extra-bright.

"Good job on the arch, bella," he whispered.

"You built it," she whispered back.

"I built a pile of sticks. You made it beautiful."

Grinning, she rested her cheek on his shoulder.

Of course, the wedding arch was a group effort—his carpentry skills, her decorations, and the florist's finishing touches—fat white peonies and deep blue cornflowers that nodded in the coastal breeze. Though she'd only met the bridal couple an hour ago, she loved knowing she contributed to their celebration.

Composed now, the brides resumed their vows, armed with tissues from the officiant, AKA Zora from the crystal shop, pulled from the pocket of her saffron Dashiki.

"Serendipity." Green Bride's clear voice carried over the murmuring waves. "That's what Zora foretold. A happy accident. I came here to repair a computer and met the love of my life." She beamed at Blue Bride. "So I promise you, my love, to keep my eyes wide open to all the serendipity before us. I promise not to get so caught up in life's little worries, or big ones, that I miss even one minute of us. Because, baby, you are the happiest accident that ever happened to me."

Beneath Danielle's cheek, Matteo's shoulder rose and fell on a shaky sigh. He squeezed her hand.

She squeezed back and exhaled a trembling breath of her own. Here she was, swimming in a big warm pool of love with a bunch of strangers and a man she barely knew. Despite everything her book club friends told her last night, despite the fortuneteller's woo-woo wisdom, despite sun and sand and surf, she knew in her heart of hearts she was being a fool. Letting herself care this much when the end was so near was hot fudge crazy sauce with stupidity sprinkles. And the longer she bathed in his loving attention, the more that ending was going to hurt. But she couldn't cut their connection now, not with Matteo's fingers laced through hers, his gentle presence holding her safe.

Seven more days.

Beneath the arch, Zora spread her arms wide. "By the powers invested in me by the State of Washington, I now pronounce you married. Smooch it up, my darlings!"

With a whoop, Green Bride lifted her new wife and spun her, sand flying. The guests cheered. Nearby beachgoers joined in, including a damp Labrador who barked joyfully and dropped his sodden tennis ball at the newlyweds' feet.

A tear spilled down Danielle's cheek—then another, and another. The combination of doggie cuteness, new love, and impending loss squeezed her ribs so tightly she could barely breathe. And of course Matteo noticed. Sweet and attentive, he noticed every detail about her, even the ones she tried to hide.

"Hey now." While the other guests drifted toward the canopy tent against the rock wall, Matteo gathered her into his arms. "What's wrong, bella?"

"It's all a bit too much." She clenched her fists, hating the wobble in her voice.

He stroked her hair. "The wedding? God, I should have thought—how long has it been?"

"Six months." Jason left the day after Christmas. She'd never forget his smug expression when he declared, "I didn't want to ruin the holiday for the kids."

Strong fingers kneaded the back of her neck. "And how long were you married?"

"Sixteen years."

"That must be so hard. And I'm an insensitive idiot." His soft lips caressed her temple.

She fisted his linen shirt. "You're not. You're wonderful."

He rocked her until the sting of memory faded, soothed by the soft swoosh of surf and the steady beat of his heart beneath her cheek. A perfect, poignant moment, all the more precious because it couldn't last.

Finally, he tipped her chin up and smoothed her damp cheeks with his thumbs. "Want me to take you home?"

Behind them, a cheer arose. She glanced over his shoulder and saw sunlight glinting off raised glasses.

"No, I want to stay." She dried her tears with her floral scarf, then took his hands. "Let's go congratulate the brides."

# Chapter Fourteen

♥

The flickering campfire gilded everything—cool sand beneath Danielle's bare feet, Matteo's wind-tossed curls, and the burnished wood of her new guitar. After a reception dinner of Hawaiian barbeque served from a food truck, the guests gathered around the fire pit to sing. She'd been slightly horrified when Matteo excused himself and returned a moment later carrying her guitar. Seems he'd conspired with her book club friends that morning, sneaking it into his SUV while Cari distracted her. But soon she relaxed into the pleasure of blending her voice with the others and strumming along with the impromptu band: three guitars, a cajon drum, and a mandolin.

The whole circle of friends and family joined in on the final chorus, a ringing, joyful noise that subsided into whoops and applause. After the newlyweds doled out a last round of hugs and waved goodbye, the revelers began to gather their belongings.

Danielle swallowed a rising bubble of melancholy as she set her guitar back in its case. "Tonight was perfect. I wish it didn't have to end. There's something magical on the beach tonight—the fire, the music, the sea..."

Matteo slid his arm around her shoulders. "The night is young, bella. There's still plenty of magic left."

After saying their goodnights, he loaded the guitar into his car, then held the door for her.

She climbed in. "What's next? You want to make out in the back seat?"

"I've got something better in mind, if you're game." He cranked the ignition and eased the SUV toward the surf line.

Her hand clamped over his knee. "What are you—"

"Notice anything about the water?"

Her grip tightened. "Only that it's getting nearer."

He chuckled and removed her clawed fingers. "It's low tide." Cutting to the right, he rounded the rock wall and pulled into their secret cove. "Look. We have the hollow to ourselves."

He hopped out and opened the rear hatch, where he flipped up a tarp to reveal a cooler, firewood, a water jug, a lantern, blankets, and...

"Is that a tent?"

He dropped the nylon bag onto the sand with a jangly thunk. "Not often the timing of the tides is this perfect." He tapped his pursed lips with his fingertip. "Must be serendipity."

She didn't know whether to kiss him or smack him. "We're spending the night?"

"If you're willing." From beneath the tarp, he pulled out a familiar gym bag and dangled it from one finger, his grin playful and slightly smug.

"How did you—?"

"Your friend Marie packed while you were getting dressed this morning. You almost walked in on her twice, but the other two steered you away."

So that's why they kept pulling her back into the bathroom to fiddle with her hair and jewelry. She smiled at the idea of her friends conspiring with Matteo. They must really like him.

He slung the bag over his shoulder. "If you'd rather not stay, that's cool. We'll still have a few hours to ourselves before the tide gets too high to drive back out." When she just gaped, he added, "Full moon tonight. Soft breezes. Starry skies." He gestured to the surrounding cliffs with a sweep of his arm. "It's a magical place at night."

He gazed out at the sea with a dreamy half-smile. "I must've been about ten last time I spent the night here. The full moon seemed so huge, like any minute it would splash into the sea. My cousin said we had to make moon magic to keep it from falling. All night long, we chanted and sang, danced in a circle, and drew symbols in the sand. It felt—I dunno. Powerful, I guess."

A whisper of moon magic caressed Danielle's skin, raising goosebumps despite the summer warmth. She stepped behind Matteo, wrapped her arms around his waist, and rested her chin on his shoulder. "Well done, moon wizard. Your magic worked."

What was he like at Noah's age? Wide-eyed and earnest, probably. Sweet, artistic, buzzing with imagination. If only she could tap into that innocence and keep her focus on this magical moment.

She nuzzled the crook of his neck. "Let's make some moon magic tonight."

He turned into her embrace, and his boyish grin outshone the moonlight. "You'll stay?"

"Absolutely." She kissed the tip of his nose.

He peppered her face with kisses, then hefted a sack of equipment. "Help me set up camp?"

Together, they wrestled the tent poles into their sockets and collected stones to weigh down the ropes. While she spread out two sleeping bags to make a double bed, he dug a small fire pit before stacking kindling and logs. Finally, he propped the folding shovel against a tall boulder several yards away. "In case nature calls during the night."

Her eyebrows rose. "Thought of everything, haven't you?"

He shrugged and flashed a sheepish grin. "You can thank my college girlfriend. Our first attempt at camping—well, let's say I under-packed. She took charge of provisions after that."

College girlfriend. No reason to flinch. He was charming, thoughtful, amazing in bed. No doubt, he'd honed those skills on a long line of former girlfriends. And no doubt, he would practice them on many lucky women to come.

Until now, Matteo hadn't mentioned his past loves. She restrained her curiosity long enough to spear marshmallows on forks while he lit the fire. Seated cross-legged, she watched the flames gild the white puffs.

He dropped down beside her and nudged her elbow. "There's Hershey bars and Graham crackers if you want s'mores."

"No thanks. I'm still stuffed from the reception." She peeled her hot, gooey marshmallow from her fork.

"Was it hard for you?" He licked melted marshmallow from his fingers. "The wedding, I mean, after your divorce?"

"Oh. No, it was lovely. Nothing like my wedding, all stuffy and formal."

Resting his elbows on his knees, Matteo gazed at her. "Why did you love him?"

She stabbed another marshmallow. "Going right for the jugular, aren't you?"

He scooted closer, his thigh warm against hers. "I just don't get why a smart woman like you would fall for a cheating asshole like him."

*Because I'm really not so smart. Exhibit A: Falling for you.*

His hand closed softly over her wrist. "You don't have to tell me if it's too painful. I didn't bring you out here to grill you." The corner of his mouth tipped. "Just marshmallows."

She gazed into those deep, dark eyes for a long moment. Dangerous eyes that drew out uncomfortable truths. "I don't mind. Gotta learn from past mistakes. That's how we grow, right?" She fiddled with her marshmallow like a tiny stress ball.

"Jason was in my study group for the world's most boring education course. He had this way of focusing his whole attention on me. Made me feel seen, you know? I loved that feeling."

Matteo's fingers softly massaged the back of her neck. "I see you, bella. Do you see me?"

She tossed her mangled marshmallow into the fire and faced him. The softness in his gaze stirred impossible longing—for a future where what she wanted mattered as much as what she owed. Where she could love a man without fearing his loss. Crazy, stupid dreams.

"I see a puzzle, Matteo. How did you end up here?"

He shrugged. "This is where I want to be."

"With a lonely older woman, when you could have someone much younger? Don't you want a family of your own?"

A tiny smile flicked across his lips, there and gone. "I have a family. Friends too. What I want is a partner. And I don't give a damn about your age. How do I make you believe that?"

*I wish I knew.* "But why are you single? You're so—" She flapped a hand. "So—everything good. It just doesn't make sense."

He sat up straighter and stared out to sea. "I was with Anna for three years. We broke up on Thanksgiving."

"She dumped you?" She squeezed his forearm. "You want me to mess her up?"

He chuckled. "It was mutual. She wanted to get married and start a family. To do that, I'd have to give up my furniture business and get a real job." His fingers hooked in air quotes around the last two words. "Something that would allow her to be a stay-at-home mom. Can't do that on the pittance I make."

"Ah." She rubbed slow circles on his back. "That sucks."

He nodded. "It does. When we started out, we were both doing creative work and barely scraping by. But we had fun. We had what we needed." He gave a sad shrug. "Over time, things changed. Anna got a promotion. Her work friends were all getting married and having babies."

"And you don't want kids?" Yet another reason their connection could never last.

He raked his fingers through his hair. "I love kids. But there are already lots of kids in my life—my nieces, my cousins' kids, my friends' kids. Hell, we're smothering the earth with too many people and too much worthless stuff."

Firelight flickered in his eyes. "That's what I love about my work. I turn old furniture into something new and useful. Good materials, quality craftsmanship, not like that pressboard crap that gets tossed into landfills every few years." He flopped onto his back, his hands laced behind his head. "I'm happy with my small-town, small-business life. In some people's eyes, that makes me a slacker."

She stretched out beside him. "Not in mine, Matteo."

He rolled toward her and twined a lock of her hair around his finger. "The question is, could I ever fit into your life? Because the thought of letting you go next Saturday is tearing me up."

A heavy weight pressed on her chest. "Matteo, I have to put my kids first."

"Of course. I'd never ask you to do otherwise." He brushed his knuckles over her cheekbone. "But don't you deserve happiness too?"

"Not at their expense." She stroked the curve of his shoulder. "I'm a teacher, Matteo. I've seen how hard it is for kids, stuck between Dad and his new girlfriend, Mom and her new boyfriend. The so-called grownups put their own desires first and ignore the effect on their kids."

He slumped back onto the sand and draped his hand over his eyes. "You don't want me to meet them."

She fought to keep her voice even as heat rose in her chest and tightened her throat. "Can't you see how stuck I am? I want to keep you and keep their lives normal, and I don't see how I can do both."

His hand closed over hers. "If anyone could pull it off, it's a mother like you who cares more about her kids' happiness than her own." With his thumb, he massaged her palm. "And maybe a guy like me. I've got first-hand experience in how parents' selfish priorities affect kids. There's no way I'll ever repeat that pattern. And I'm not looking to disrupt your kids' lives. I'm just a guy who met the most amazing woman and wants to hold on to her." He drew her hand to his lips. "Give us a chance, bella."

If any man could make her want to risk her heart, it was Matteo. But to risk her kids' hearts, she'd need a lot more than pretty promises. Building that kind of trust takes time—time she and Matteo didn't have. She sniffed and swiped at her tear-prickled eyes. "You're merciless, you know that?"

He rolled to his feet and tugged her up with him. "Good name for a pirate, eh? Matteo the Merciless." Flashing a wicked grin, he shuffled backward toward the tent. "Climb aboard? I promise to leave my blade at the door."

Seven more days. Six more nights.

Each night with Matteo would only make parting that much more painful, but a night together under the stars was too enticing to miss. She kicked off her sandals, ducked inside, and sank onto the pile of bedding. "Pretty cushy for a tent."

"But wait, there's more." He unzipped a panel, leaving only mesh between them and the stars.

"A tent with a moon roof? What a delicious surprise." She pecked his lips, then lay back and drank in the diamond-dusted sky.

He settled beside her, his head cushioned on his bent arm, and studied her with a heavy-lidded gaze. "Delicious surprise." His husky voice raised goosebumps, but he didn't touch her. He just rested there, inches away, watching her watch the stars.

His breath against her cheek sent tingles sparkling over her skin. Wood smoke and burnt sugar blended with his signature scent of sandalwood and salt air. She closed her eyes and breathed deeply. Desire and pleasure swirled low in her belly.

His lips skimmed the shell of her ear, and cascading shivers tightened her skin as he trailed soft, slow kisses down her throat and over her shoulder. She arched her throat when his soft curls brushed beneath her chin, then between her breasts. His fingertips whispered over the thin cotton of her bodice, and she squirmed, craving more. But he teased her with the lightest touch, skating over her breasts, her waist, her sides, her hips, never nearing the pulsing center that burned for him.

Panting now, she grasped his wrist and tugged his hand downward. "Please, Matteo."

"Hush, bella," he whispered. "If I only have six more nights with you, I want to make the most of each moment."

So he'd been counting too. Sharp regret sliced through the pleasure. Biting her lip, she turned away.

"Stay with me, love." He cupped her cheek and turned her face back to his. His eyes glinted in the near darkness, and the moonlight tipped his hair with silver. "Let me see you. Let me know you."

Emotion swelled in her chest. She filled her lungs with cool night air—and relaxed.

"There you are." Finally, he took her mouth in a deep, sensual exploration that went on and on. She closed her eyes and sank into his kiss, the stars overhead eclipsed by the sparkles dancing behind her lids as she clutched his back and rocked her hips against his.

He drew back with a rumbly laugh that vibrated her bones. "Slow down, bella. Make it last." He sat up and pulled his shirt over his head. His crisp chinos remained in place, though, despite her pout. When he lay beside her again, she glided greedy hands over his skin, warm and smooth over firm muscle.

He fumbled with the back of her wrap dress. "How does this thing open?"

"Here." She guided him to the tie at her waist. Soon he had her unwrapped, shivering more from anticipation than from the evening chill.

Warm flannel beneath her, heated skin above. Warm breath, plush lips, whispers and murmurs. Each time urgent desire swelled, he lightened his touch until her breathing calmed and her pulse quieted. Over and over, he coaxed her to a high plateau and held her there, trembling. Pleasure soaked every nerve, every inch of her skin as she floated, content to be guided, molded by his touch. All the while, his hips rocked gently against her, echoing the whisper of the surf.

He caressed her for what seemed like days, his murmured endearments dissolving into soft moans and endless repetitions of her name. At last, he stripped bare and moved against her, the brush of his soft body hair exquisitely arousing.

A foil wrapper crinkled, and then the blunt head of his cock nudged her slick opening. Her breath caught, then rushed out as he entered her with one deep thrust. In and out he glided, their bodies undulating, swimming through a sea of pleasure, up, up, up toward sparkling sunlight. With a gasp, they broke the surface together—one thundering heartbeat, one triumphant cry.

Afterward, no words. Just the rise and fall of his chest against hers, his soft sigh as he withdrew and disposed of the condom. He pulled the top sleeping bag over them, twined his arms and legs around her, and pressed a kiss to her temple. Warm, sated, safe, she drifted into sleep.

A full bladder woke her sometime later. Carefully extricating herself from his embrace, she found the lantern, pulled Matteo's shirt over her bare skin, and unzipped the tent fly. Business taken care of, she stepped through night-cool sand, silky beneath her feet, back toward their shelter. She paused a moment to watch the moon, hovering just above the line where sea meets sky. Its reflected light carved a silvery path to this secluded spot she shared with Matteo. The waves whispered and sighed. As the night breeze lifted her hair, a thought materialized—not once since entering that tent had she thought about Jason, about her kids, about the end of this connection. Wrapped in Matteo's love, she'd finally mastered the art of living in the present, if only for a night.

# Chapter Fifteen

♥

Danielle woke to the scent of coffee. Rolling onto her back, she stretched and grinned. After years of being the one who did all the planning, Matteo's pampering was something she could get used to. Addicted to, even.

She dug into the overnight bag Marie packed and thanked the gods for her friend's attention to detail. She found wet wipes to remove the smeared remnants of yesterday's make-up and the stickiness from their lovemaking, plus lip gloss and cologne, her toothbrush and toothpaste. After a quick clean-up, she pulled on a long-sleeved U Dub T-shirt and shorts, then ventured outside.

Still empty but for their campsite and a few inquisitive seagulls, the beach was quiet in the early-morning light. She inhaled deeply and released a contented sigh.

Barefoot, in faded cutoffs and a Seahawks hoodie, Matteo squatted over a small camp stove that held an enamel coffee pot and a frying pan. The sight of him all bed-rumpled made her heart swell.

She cleared her throat. "Good morning."

He hopped to his feet—his agility a reminder of how damn young he was.

"Good morning, bella. Did you sleep well? Are you hungry? Ready for breakfast? We've got eggs, smoked salmon, ciabatta bread, melon—"

She held a finger to his lips. "First, I'd like this." She wound her arms around his neck and kissed him. "Last night was amazing. Thank you."

His lashes lowered, and he pulled her closer. "I'll never forget it. Thanks for trusting me."

He was right. Last night, something had shifted between them. She'd placed herself in his hands, let him set the pace, and he'd read her reactions with skill and sensitivity. More than anything, she longed to hang onto this warm, easy connection. But how?

He released her and poured a mug of coffee, then stirred in a stream of sugar. "Black and sweet, right?" He went back to the stove and waved a spatula. "The tide left lots of shells. Go ahead, explore. I'll call you when it's ready."

She returned to the tent for her phone. Coffee in hand, she strolled the length of the little beach and snapped photos to share with her kids—tiny crabs battling over a half-eaten fish, bubbles swirling around her toes, and a pair of sharp-eyed seagulls who stayed a few flaps ahead in case snacks might appear, not unlike her own always-hungry offspring.

With a sigh, she gazed up and down the shoreline, then back at Matteo, humming as he cracked eggs into the skillet. A smile curved her lips. Olivia and Noah would love this. They would love him.

She sucked in a bracing breath of sea air and let it take shape, the plan that had been dancing around the edge of her awareness since she awoke.

Jason had the kids every other weekend and on Wednesday nights. She'd spend that time with Matteo. If things were still looking up at the end of the summer, she would introduce him to the kids.

Icy surf washed over her toes, and a drop splashed onto her phone screen. She wiped it away, uploaded the photos, composed a quick text, and pressed Send. Nothing.

She tapped again and squinted at the screen. No bars. But a new text had arrived during the night. Olivia.

> **Dad and Sharla are still fighting, and her kids are total turd-wads. Can we come home?**

A wave of nausea washed through her. While she'd been rolling around the tent with Matteo, her children had been trying to reach her. She tossed the coffee and sprinted back to their campsite.

Matteo stood and grinned. "Almost ready."

"We have to go. Now."

He dropped the spatula and grasped her arms. "Bella, what's wrong?"

She showed him Olivia's text. "No signal out here." Angry tears prickled her eyes. "My kids need me, and I can't reach them."

"Okay, okay." He glanced toward the surf line. "Tide will be low enough to drive through in an hour or so."

She fixed him with a bug-eyed glare. "An hour?"

Matteo raked a hand through his bed-mussed hair, ran to the tent, and returned wearing battered canvas shoes. "Give me your phone."

"Code's 1829." She slapped it into his palm, and he jogged toward the wall of boulders separating them from the main beach, calling over his shoulder, "Turn off the stove." He scrambled up the rocks, held her phone aloft, shook his head and hollered something, but the surf swallowed his words. Picking his way carefully, he climbed higher, lifted the phone again, and flashed a thumbs-up.

Driven by pure Mama Bear adrenaline, she sprinted toward him, heedless of the sharp shells and stones jabbing her bare feet. She hoisted herself up onto the first boulder.

Matteo waved her off. "It's too steep. Tell me what you want to say, and I'll send a text."

Her phone rang. Startled, she slipped and cursed as jagged barnacles ripped a gash on her shin. Blood welled and dripped.

"Bella!" He started toward her.

She stabbed a finger at him. "Answer it."

He huffed, but he did as he was told. "Hello? She, uh, can't come to the phone right now...A friend of your mom's. You okay? Your brother too?"

Time slowed to a crawl as he nodded and grunted several uh-huhs. Her mind raced from one worst-case scenario to the next. Finally, he scrubbed his hand down his face. "Okay. I'll tell her." He tucked the phone in his hip pocket and leveled a thunderous glare. "Stay where you are. I'm coming down."

"Matteo, damn it." Wincing, she scooted down to the beach, ripping her shorts in the process, and limped toward the water.

He hopped onto the sand, and without saying a word, scooped her up in his arms.

"Wait. What did she say?"

"They're boarding a plane. She'll call you when they land," he said through clenched teeth. "Your daughter sounds as stubborn as you."

A flush of pride heated her cheeks.

He deposited her into a camp chair and darted to his SUV, returning with the first aid kit. She peppered him with questions while he washed her wound, then applied antiseptic ointment and a gauze bandage.

"Are they flying alone?"

"No. With Dad."

"He's bringing them to his place?"

"I didn't ask. He was busy yelling at the gate agent."

That sounded like him. "Shit. I'll have to pack up and hit the road."

"Bella, no!" He gripped her ankle, breathing hard through flared nostrils.

Stunned at his sudden anger, she held her breath.

He softened his grip and stroked her calf. "He made this mess. Let him take responsibility for fixing it."

Her brow contracted. "Matteo, you don't have kids. You don't know how it feels. Jason's a selfish, unreliable ass. I have to be the responsible one. I have no choice."

He sank back onto his heels, covered his face, and huffed a huge sigh. When he finally dropped his hands, the defeat in his gaze twisted her guts. "All right. You rest here while I pack up." He moved to the stove and scraped scrambled eggs onto a tin plate. "At least eat something. Sounds like you're gonna need your strength."

"I'm not hungry," she grumbled.

"Me neither." Mouth twisted in a grimace, he tossed the eggs onto the sand. While he broke camp, the seagulls feasted.

He loaded up his Subaru, drove down to the surf line, and waited until an outgoing wave receded, then gunned it around the point. Neither spoke until he dropped her at her rental house and insisted on walking her to the door.

"Still no word?" he asked, brow rumpled.

She shook her head, not trusting her voice. It would wobble. So would her chin. And the tears surging behind her lids would overflow. She didn't want their last moment to end this way. She didn't want it to end at all.

Matteo stroked the backs of his fingers down her cheek. "Listen, bella. This isn't goodbye. Just an interruption." His voice wavered, and he sniffed hard before pressing his forehead to hers. "Promise me you'll call as soon as you sort this out?"

She nodded, and a tear dribbled down her cheek.

He brushed it away with his thumb, pressed a quick, hard kiss to her lips, and spun away.

She held it together until his car rounded the corner. Once he was out of sight, she folded onto the stairs and wept.

# Chapter Sixteen

♥

Danielle pulled into her driveway, unloaded a huge haul of groceries, and—for the thousandth time—rechecked her phone. After a two-hour delay, the kids' flight landed in Sea-Tac at one, and a mile-long text chain began. Seems they browbeat their dad into driving them straight to Trappers Cove since their promised SoCal beach vacation had been cut short. They'd get their traditional family Fourth of July after all. Minus Jason, of course. As far as she was concerned, Jason could go pound sand, as long as he pounded it far away from her.

Danielle nibbled a nail. They should be here any minute now. No reason to be nervous—just another hand-off between divorced parents. Her new reality. She'd already made up their bedrooms, noted times and locations for all the 4th of July events, and straightened up the house after her book club's visit. What she hadn't done was tell Matteo.

This sudden change blew her cautious, rational plan all to hell. They were bound to bump into Matteo in town, or else one of the many locals she'd met would see them, and the news would get back to him. He was already hurt by this situation—she couldn't add to his pain by keeping secrets. Even if their affair proved impossible to hold, she owed him this call.

So why was she sitting on the deck, staring blankly at families streaming to and from the beach? Her phone pinged in her hand. Noah's number.

> **Be there in fifteen**

She gulped several deep breaths, then texted Matteo.

> **Jason's bringing the kids here**

No response. Must be busy at the gelato shop. Shaky with nerves, she paced the length of the deck. Much as she'd like to ream Jason out, she couldn't do it in front of the kids. They'd been through enough the past few days.

A moment later, Jason's Lexus rounded the corner and pulled into her driveway. Though it'd only been a week since she hugged them goodbye, a bubble of emotion blocked her throat and pushed tears to her eyes when the kids tumbled out and charged up the stairs.

"God, I missed you guys." She folded them into her arms and inhaled their kid scent—sweat and sweets and fruity shampoo.

Bouncing on his toes, Noah chattered a mile a minute. "Missed you too, Mom. Look, we got Velociraptor hats. This dude on the plane worked on two *Jurassic Park* movies! CGI stuff. So cool! I totally wanna learn that. Dad says he'll get me a better computer."

She grasped his shoulders and gave him the suspicious mama once-over. His sandy hair was travel-mussed but clean, and his cheeks and nose glowed bright pink.

"Forgot your sunscreen?"

He shrugged. "No one reminded me."

Olivia sucked her teeth. "Did so, baby bro. Every. Single. Day."

Noah snorted and shoved his sister's shoulder. "You're not my mom."

"No, but I am. Go get your bags."

Jostling and giggling, the kids trotted to the car, where Jason lifted bags from the trunk. He looked the same—handsome in a WASP-y way, though his blond hair was thinning on top. In his powder blue polo and chinos, he'd be right at home on a golf course or at a corporate picnic.

Funny, their last face-to-face meeting left her weepy for hours, still mourning what they'd lost. Now? All she felt was irritation over his shitty judgment.

He loaded the kids with suitcases and shopping bags, then pulled out several more and started up the stairs.

She planted herself in his path. "Whoa. How much crap did you buy them?"

He kept his ice-blue gaze down. "Too much. It's what divorced dads do, right?" He flashed her a half-smile she once found charming. Still nada. Interesting. "This is my stuff."

Her mouth went Sahara dry. "Your stuff?"

He set down his bags and closed his eyes for a moment. "Look, Dani, I know I screwed up. I didn't mean to leave you stuck with the cost of this rental. Let me pay half, and we can give the kids a nice 4th of July, just like we always—"

"Have you lost what's left of your mind?" She darted a glance at the house to make sure their kids were out of hearing range.

Jason's lips thinned in that smarmy, I-know-what's-best expression that made her jaw clench. "I'll take Olivia's room. She can bunk with you."

"No." She shoved a suitcase with her foot. "Take your stuff and go."

His gaze tightened. "Don't you want what's best for the kids? After that mess with Sharla's boys, they need some normalcy in their lives."

"Are you flippin' kidding me?" Her eyebrows reached for her hairline. "You caused this mess, Mr. Can't-keep-it-in-his-pants. And this—" She waved a hand toward the house. "This is our new normal, thanks to you. Separate vacations. Separate lives. Sharing the house would give the kids hope that we're getting back together." Glowering, she poked his sternum, hard. "And that is not ever happening. Now go home."

"You need help, bella?"

Both their heads snapped toward the sidewalk, where Matteo stood holding a paper bag. Sharp steel glinted behind his casual half-smile. "I brought gelato for your kids. Limoncello and pistachio, right?" He took a stepforward and held out the bag. "And amarena for you." His gaze darted from her to Jason.

Well, shit. This was not at all how she wanted to handle this situation, but...What did her mama always say? *It is what it is, darling. Don't mope, act.*

Like a wet Labrador, she shimmied the tension off her shoulders and trotted down the stairs. "Thank you, Matteo. That's very thoughtful of you." She took the bag, linked her arm through his, and faced her ex. "Jason, this is my friend Matteo." Just to be mean, she stroked Matteo's firm biceps.

Jason gaped. "Your—friend?"

Taking his cue, Matteo kissed her temple. "You okay here?" he murmured.

"I will be. Come on, I want you to meet my kids." She led him up the stairs, past her spluttering ex.

When she opened the screen door, both little lurkers sprang backwards, eyes wide.

This was it. Her future with Matteo would turn on this moment. She smoothed the tension from her voice. "Olivia, Noah, I want you to meet my new friend. You remember Sal from the gelato shop? Matteo is his nephew."

Olivia's startled expression eased toward a knowing grin. "Wow. Um, pleased to meet you, Matteo."

Noah only had eyes for the paper bag. "You brought us ice cream?"

"Yeah. Should I dish it up?" He moved toward the kitchen.

The screen door slammed open. Red-faced, Jason snarled, "Kids, outside."

She raised her hand palm out, like a traffic cop. "No, go get your gelato. Your dad and I will discuss this outside." She shot Jason a sharp glance. "Like grown-ups."

On the deck, Jason lost his shit, alternately flapping his hands and clasping his skull as if the top might fly off. "So this is why you don't want me to stay? You've been sharing the house with that gigolo? That's a fine example for your children."

A veil of calm determination descended. "You've got nothing to say about it, Jason. You left me, remember? I don't have to put my life on hold for you. And no, Matteo won't be staying with us, but he is a part of my life now."

Jason glared for a long moment, then stomped to the door and hollered, "Kids, come on. We'll go to the Freedom Fair in Tacoma. There's an air show, fireworks—it'll be fun."

Clutching their ice cream bowls, the kids conferred in low tones. Noah spoke up. "Naw, Dad. We had fun with you and Sharla, but now we're gonna stay with Mom. We'll see you when we get back."

Relief fizzed through her veins. The moment she'd been dreading was over. "They'll call you every day, Jason. Right, kids?"

"Totally," Olivia answered. "Just like we did with Mom."

*Take that, vacation stealer.*

Because her kids were watching, she bit back a grin of triumph until Jason tossed his bags into his car and drove off.

# Chapter Seventeen

♥

Matteo gently gripped Noah's shoulder. "Right shin against the rim?"

He nodded, his pale curls bouncing. "Check."

"Bend low at the hips?"

Noah hinged forward. "Check."

"Eyes on the forty?"

"Check."

Matteo backed away. "Drumroll, please."

Danielle and Olivia trilled their tongues while Matteo drummed on a trash can. Noah blew out a breath through pursed lips, then launched. The Skee-ball rolled smoothly as butter up the lane and into the forty-point hoop. With a kerchunk, kerchunk, the machine spit out a long stream of tickets, which Noah snatched up and waved overhead, hooting with glee.

"Bravo, piccolo," Matteo crowed. "Almost as good as your sister."

Noah's forehead rumpled. "Bull dookie!" He grabbed for his sister's strip of tickets, but she tucked them behind her back.

Danielle hid her grin behind Matteo's broad shoulder. "Go on, pick your prizes."

Squabbling and jostling, the kids made their way to the prize counter at the back of the crowded, noisy arcade.

Taking advantage of their diverted attention, Danielle pulled Matteo in for a juicy smooch. "Thanks, Coach."

He chuckled and wrapped his arms around her. "Advantage of growing up in a beach town. Mad Skee-ball skills."

"And go-karts. And bumper cars. And...what else? We've been to so many places I've lost track."

"Don't forget the secret collection at Souvenir Galaxy."

She shuddered. "That was seriously creepy. I swear, that mummified mermaid thing is a shaved monkey with a salmon tail."

"Heresy! Hush your mouth, woman." He kissed her again. And again.

She squirmed from his grip. "The kids will see."

"Give them some credit, bella. They're smart. They know what's up." He glanced back at the prize counter, where Olivia was collecting a plush panda.

"Yeah, I guess so." Her kids' easy acceptance of Matteo surprised and delighted her. Then again, they'd already been conditioned by their dad's revolving stable of girlfriends. It seemed they were sturdier than she thought.

She squeezed Matteo's waist. "You've been a champ, giving up all your free time to entertain my offspring."

He squeezed back. "Well, I do have ulterior motives. I know you have to get back home for their soccer league, but I'm hoping you'll let me come up for a few games." He nuzzled her neck. "Especially when they're staying with their dad."

It would be a long time before she trusted her ex again, but Matteo was right. Jason was a grown-ass man, and he had to forge his own relationship with the kids now, independent of hers. At least she trusted Olivia and Noah to tell her when Jason's screw-ups became too onerous.

Matteo jerked a thumb toward the door. "Gotta get back to Sal soon. I'll text you after we close up."

"We'll have the food ready by then. Your friends still holding a place for us on the beach?"

He nodded. "Got a prime spot. They've been camping out there since this morning. Just bring folding chairs and blankets. It'll cool off tonight." He snuggled closer. "Unfortunately, we can't duck into the tent and warm up like we did the other night."

She stifled a laugh. "My kids would be scandalized."

He kissed her forehead and fixed her with a gaze that warmed her all the way through. "You're a great mom, Danielle. Fun, but firm." He gave her butt a quick squeeze, drawing a squeak. "You know, Trappers Cove is a great place to raise kids. When the tourists leave, there's still a tight-knit community here. Pretty good school. We've even got a soccer league. And kids who need a speech therapist."

"How would you know that?"

He lowered his gaze and shuffled his feet. "Friend of Sal's on the school board."

She laced her fingers through his and sighed. Two weeks ago, she'd have scoffed at the idea of pulling up stakes and moving to a little shore town. Now, the idea was mighty appealing. A smaller house to maintain, smaller mortgage payments too, a slower pace, and daily walks on the beach with Matteo. Not to mention nightly cuddles, waking up to his warm, sleepy-soft body wrapped around hers...

*Head out of the clouds, Delfino.*

She shook her head. "If it were just up to me, I'd put in my job application tomorrow. But—" she waved toward the back of the arcade. "They get a say too."

"Fair enough." He folded her against his chest and rocked her, moving to their own slow rhythm despite the frantic dings and clangs all around them.

Close behind her, someone snorted. She turned, expecting to see Olivia's teen sneer, but the intruder was a vaguely familiar young woman, arms crossed, nose wrinkled.

"Well, well, well. Matteo's still hanging onto his cougar. Thought you'da dumped her old ass by now."

A flash of black and white bounced off the critic's head as Olivia wielded her new stuffed panda like a club. "That's right, he's with my mom. And she's way cuter than you." She waggled her fingers in that infuriatingly dismissive manner only a teen girl can master. "So move along now. Buh-bye."

The young woman flounced away. Noah trotted up, a plush green snake wrapped around his shoulders. "What'd I miss?"

Eyes crinkled in laughter, Matteo said, "Just your sister being a badass." He fist-bumped Olivia. "Respect, Princess. Well, guys, I've gotta go. See you on the beach tonight."

He shot Danielle a look of longing as he backed away.

Noah huffed. "It's okay, man. You can kiss her in front of us. We won't hurl."

"Just, like, no tongue, okay?" Olivia added.

Giggling, Danielle grasped Matteo's shoulders and gave him her first kid-approved smooch.

With a laugh and a wave, he made his way through the crowd.

She wrapped her arm around Olivia. "Thanks, kiddo. That was awesome."

Olivia shrugged. "Who knows? I might want a younger boyfriend someday." She counted on her fingers. "Let's see. Eleven years younger. That means he's—two!"

Noah socked her arm. "Eew, you perv."

Danielle separated them. "All right, enough violence. Where to next?"

"I'm hungry," Noah declared.

"You're always hungry." Grinning over her incredibly good luck, Danielle led her little family back onto the crowded street. Until her ex's ill-timed arrival in Trappers Cove, she'd envisioned a future where fun times like this would be shared with either her kids or with Matteo, but—fingers crossed—Noah and Olivia seemed at ease with her new...

"Boyfriend," she whispered, giddy with happiness.

"What's that, Mom?" As sharp-eared as a bat, Olivia snatched that clue.

"Beautiful, I said." Danielle slung her arm around her daughter's skinny shoulders and smooched the top of her head. "I'm so glad you guys stayed for the holiday."

Noah linked his arm through her free one and tugged them toward the cluster of food vendors further down Main Street. "Dad's a poop-head on the fourth. Never wants to stay up to see the fireworks."

She really ought to scold her son for disparaging his father that way, but Noah was right—Jason was a poophead. And for once, she got to enjoy being the fun parent. What a treat!

Trappers Cove had pulled out all the stops for the Fourth of July. Balloons bobbed everywhere. Red, white, and blue bunting hung from the old-fashioned streetlamps, and buskers and vendors filled the sidewalks. All along Main Street, visitors streamed from shop to shop and clustered around booths hawking crafts, beach gear, and food.

"I smell corn dogs." Noah launched himself into the crowd.

Fortified with cheese-stuffed corn dogs, the kids scanned the other offerings on this block. "Look, a fortuneteller. Can we, Mom?" Olivia's teenaged cool fell away as she hopped, hands clasped over her chest.

In front of her crystal shop, Zora had set up a canopy draped with glittery scarves. Striking in her purple caftan and campy jeweled turban, she inspected the palm of a girl about Olivia's age. After sending her customer on her way, Zora beckoned to Danielle.

"Good to see you again, dear. Are these angels yours?"

Noah's eyes bugged out. Clearly, knowing a psychic netted Mom some serious cool points.

She introduced her children, dropped a ten into the jar, then backed off as they seated themselves at Zora's table. "I'll just check out that stained-glass stand."

She kept an eye on them, of course, smiling at their wide-eyed expressions as Zora foretold their futures. A few minutes later, the kids returned, gesticulating, heads bent close.

"Must've been an interesting prediction," Danielle observed.

Noah went first. "She said I would find treasure on the beach. Do we have a shovel?"

Olivia clucked her tongue. "It's a metaphor, numbnuts."

"Language, Olivia. What your sister means is that treasure could be anything valuable."

He nodded. "Uh, okay. Like money? Or jewelry? I'll bet people drop all kinds of stuff on the beach."

"And what's your prediction, Olivia?"

"It was weird. She said not to be scared of open doors."

Danielle tapped her pursed lips. "That's a thinker." *And not so different from what Zora told me.* "So, ready to help me grill some chicken for tonight?"

Following the kids through the crowd, she chuckled at the sweet irony. First the school board, then the fortuneteller. Matteo was rallying the troops to convince her to stay. If only it were that easy.

Back in the kitchen, Noah shucked corn while Olivia diced peppers for pasta salad.

Noah scooped corn silk from the sink into the trash can. "Man, I love it here. I wish we could live here all the time."

Open doors. She snuck a glance at her daughter, whose lips were clamped tight.

"No way." Olivia gave her head a sharp shake. "All my friends are in Tacoma."

Danielle's stomach sank. That's what she got for allowing herself to fantasize. It would be years before she could reconcile her obligation to her kids and her desire to be with Matteo full time.

Olivia's soft hand fell on her shoulder. "You're not gonna ask us to move, are you?"

She should've bought that crystal Zora recommended for wisdom and balance. "No, baby, I'm not going to ask you to move. Not anytime soon, anyway. But I will want to come here more often."

Noah folded and unfolded a strip of corn husk. "Are you gonna marry Matteo?"

Her heart pinched as she drank in Olivia's tight-lipped expression, Noah's nervous, fiddly fingers. So young, so at the mercy of her decision.

"Matteo and I just met two weeks ago. It's way too early to talk about marriage."

Both kids exhaled.

"I really like him, though, and I want to keep seeing him. I don't know if we'll end up together long term or not. I hope we will. But you guys always come first."

Noah grinned. "That's cool. I like him too, way better than Sharla."

"Sharla's okay," Olivia added. "Not as nice as Matteo, but she's not mean or anything." She exchanged a look with her brother. "But her sons are dickwads."

Noah nodded. "Total douche waffles."

She held up a hand. "Hey, hey, where's this language coming from?"

Oliva tsked. "We're not babies, Mom. And don't worry. We're not gonna turn into Brayden and Jayden if you hook up with Matteo." She cocked a hip. "Lots of my friends' parents are divorced. Right, bro?"

"At least half. Hey—" he clutched a handful of corn husks. "Matteo doesn't have kids, does he?"

"Nope." She grabbed a kitchen towel from the counter and flicked it at each of them. "Now, let's get this chicken on the grill."

While the chicken sizzled, she snuck glances at the kids, flopped on their bellies on the chaise cushions, snort-laughing over videos on Olivia's phone. Love for them swelled her chest and filled her eyes with happy tears. They really were great kids, and even if their new normal didn't resemble their old life, they were going to be okay.

"We're all going to be okay," she whispered to the brilliant blue sky.

# Chapter Eighteen

Good thing Matteo's friends had saved them a spot because cars and trucks lined up on the hard-packed sand, and the rest of the beach was a patchwork of blankets, towels, and tents with hardly any room to walk, much less stretch out.

Snuggled together on their beach blanket, Danielle and Matteo watched the fireworks grand finale blossom and boom. Olivia, Noah, and the half-dozen kids attached to their group hooted Oohs and Aahs with each new burst.

With a dreamy smile, Danielle leaned onto Matteo's broad shoulder. "We did exactly the same thing when I was a kid."

"Us too." He chuckled. "But back then, I wasn't remembering a certain night in a tent with a certain lady." He kissed her hair. "Talk about fireworks, bella. Kapow."

Her body heated at the reminder. Since the kids' arrival, she and Matteo had to settle for clandestine groping. No matter how cool they seemed with the idea of Mom dating, she wasn't ready to sleep with Matteo under the same roof as her kids. And man, was she feeling the lack.

"Cowabunga!" Noah dove down beside them, spraying sand everywhere. "That was great. Is there any food left?"

Danielle pointed. "Go ask Jerry. He's in charge of the grill."

He was halfway to his feet when Matteo stopped him. "Fix yourself a plate, and get your sister, okay? I want to talk to you guys."

Noah cocked his head to the side, then shrugged and trotted off.

Goosebumps prickled her skin. "Matteo, what—?"

He patted her knee. "Don't worry, I'm not gonna propose." He winked. "Not tonight, anyway."

She prodded him, but he only grinned and pulled her in for another far-too-chaste kiss.

A few moments later, Noah returned with a hot dog, a mound of potato salad, and his sister, who eyed Matteo as if he might bite. She dropped onto the blanket. "What's up?"

Matteo's grip on Danielle's hand tightened. He gave her a soft, private smile, then faced the kids. "So, uh, I know you guys have to go back soon. Summer soccer league starts next week, right?"

Noah held up a finger. "Yeah, about that—"

"Let me finish, okay?" Matteo sucked in a breath. "I have to stay here and help my Zio Sal with the shop. But I talked to Sal, and his guest room is yours whenever you want it."

Olivia wrinkled her nose. "All three of us in one room? Eew."

He chuckled. "I was hoping your mom would stay upstairs with me." He squeezed Danielle's hand again. "The thing is, I'm in love with her."

Her heart karate-kicked her ribs.

Eyebrows sky-high, the kids gawked at each other, then at her.

She forced her lungs to inflate. "Matteo, I—"

"Still not finished." He raised her hand to his lips and kissed it. "So I want you guys to know I'm not trying to replace your dad or anything. I'm not trying to rearrange your lives either."

Slow nods from the kids.

Matteo's bright-eyed gaze held hers as he finished his obviously rehearsed speech. "I just want to spend as much time as possible with her. And with you guys, if you'll let me."

A juicy sniff burst through Danielle's blurry, stunned state. She snapped her head toward Olivia, who swiped away a tear.

"Aww. That's so sweet." She elbowed her brother. "Isn't that sweet, Noah?"

He shrugged. "I guess."

Another sharp jab.

"I mean, that's cool with me. Especially since we're not playing soccer this summer."

His sister nodded. "Right."

Still reeling from Matteo's declaration, she wheeled on the kids. "Since when? Your dad already paid and—"

Apparently, this was Interrupt Danielle Night, because Olivia jumped right in. "So Noah and me were talking on the plane."

"Dad was asleep," Noah interjected. "He was snoring so loud this lady in the next row kept giving us the stink eye."

Olivia glared at him. "Anyway, since we both play sports during the school year, we thought it would be cool to just, you know, chill during the summer."

"Especially at the beach," Noah added with a grin, as if the whole brilliant plan had been his idea. Had it? Or were her kids and Matteo in cahoots?

Danielle forced her shoulders down from their ear-level perch. "Um, why don't you guys go hang out with your friends for a while? I need to talk to Matteo."

They hopped to their feet and trotted away, but before Danielle could open her mouth, Olivia dashed back, talking a mile a minute. "I almost forgot. Emma and Jayce are having a sleepover in their backyard tonight. Can we go? Pleasepleaseplease?"

Matteo nudged her ribs. "Jerry and Lana's kids. I can vouch for the parents. They live right next door to Sal."

Okay, definitely in cahoots. "I'll think about it. Give me a minute."

The kids scooted back to their new friends. Danielle sank onto the blanket, flopped onto her back, and blinked up at the stars. Matteo reclined next to her, propped on his elbow, and twirled a lock of her hair around his finger. For several minutes, they lay side by side as bottle rockets and firecrackers exploded up and down the beach. The sharp scent of gunpowder filled the air and made her eyes tear, but she kept her gaze on the heavens while her mind spun and fizzed.

*He loves me. He's in love with me.* She turned it over and over, not quite able to grasp the shape of it, the heft and color and taste of this amazing...serendipity?

She hadn't allowed herself to believe this could be possible. No matter how sweet their union, no matter how high she flew in his arms, how easily she laughed with him and walked with him and shared cozy silence, she'd been bracing herself for the pain of goodbye.

Matteo leaned into her field of vision and wiped the dampness from her cheek. "Talk to me, bella."

A laugh burbled up. "Is this real? Or was there something funny in those brownies?"

His hopeful expression crumpled. "Damn. I screwed the pooch, didn't I?" He sat up and hugged his knees. "I thought, since your kids will be impacted, I'd better tell them too." He dropped his head onto his folded arms. "I feel like that guy who proposed on the Jumbotron and got turned down."

She pushed upright and hugged him, resting her cheek on his hunched shoulder. "No, bello, you didn't screw the pooch. You did exactly right."

Slowly, he straightened and faced her. "Really?"

"Yeah." It was difficult to speak through her mile-wide grin. "Telling the kids was so thoughtful of you. And sweet. And perfect." She stroked his cheek. "And I love you too." She sniffled hard. "Crazy, right? We've only known each other for two weeks."

His smile shone brighter than the fireworks, brighter than the stars, brighter than anything she'd dared hope for. "When it's right, it's right. Sono pazzo di te." He pressed his lips to hers.

"Wait," she murmured into his kiss. "I know that one. You're, um..."

He smiled into their kiss. "Crazy about you, bella."

"Mom, they're packing up. Can we go?"

She looked up to find Noah beside his sister, wiggling like a puppy. Clearly, seeing their mom kissing a new guy was not the traumatic experience she'd feared.

Olivia wheedled, "C'mon, please? The parents will be there. They're Matteo's friends."

He chuckled against her temple. "We'll be able to see them from my balcony."

She raised her hands in surrender. "Okay, okay. Let's go."

Together, they packed up their gear and walked, arm in arm, through cool sand and fireworks-toasted ocean breeze, into the first night of their new life.

Thanks for reading! Read on for more *Trappers Cove* books and other series by Sadira Stone. But first...

Reviews are the life blood of hard-working authors like me, so if you enjoyed *Sweet Summer Surprise*, I'd be so thrilled and grateful if you'd leave a review. Even a line or two about what you enjoyed helps so much! Just find the book's retail page on your favorite online bookseller's site and find "Leave/Write a Customer Review" – usually located near the stars or book title. There's a link below to get you started. Thank you from the bottom of my heart! Extra virtual smooches for reviews on Goodreads and Bookbub

**Don't miss the next** *Trappers Cove Romance*, **coming July 2025 –** *Kieran's Light: A Midlife Beach Town Halloween Romance*

*A ghostly encounter transforms a Halloween fling into a life-changing about-face.*

Battle-scarred Army surgeon Addy Connor faces an agonizing choice. Will she continue her military career despite unrelenting PTSD, or return to her stifling hometown to care for her venomous mother—or dare to reinvent her life?

After surviving an oil rig disaster, Kieran O'Malley has finally found peace as Trappers Cove's lighthouse keeper. But the nightmares are returning, triggered by his passion for a beautiful military doctor whose struggles are so like his own.

Together, they confront haunting memories and a legendary ghost. Can these two wounded birds learn to fly again, or is their fiery fling doomed to crash?

**Check out the rest of the** *Trappers Cove* **series!**

***Passion in the Cards: An Opposites-Attract Metaphysical Beach Town Romance*** (novella)

Headstrong, homebody farmer clashes with freedom-loving hippie chick, but their blazing chemistry is unstoppable. Though Jesse knows bewitching fortuneteller Gemma will never settle down in their quirky beach town, he can't resist playing with fire. When a harmless secret backfires, Gemma discovers just how deeply she's wounded Jesse, and how desperately she wants to keep him.

***Passionate Brew: An Enemies-to-Lovers Beach Town Brewery Romance*** (novella)

When a control-freak brewery owner is forced to partner with a prickly master brewer, their business and their hearts will never be the same. Working side by side ignites sizzling desire. But when a high-stakes craft beer competition arouses their fierce rivalry, can new love survive this battle of wills? Come to Trappers Cove for a sizzling enemies-to-lovers small town workplace romance.

### _The Billionaire's Christmas Castle: A Silver Fox Holiday Beach Town Romance_(novel)

His billions can't buy what he craves most—her love. Can a spoiled tycoon and a fiercely independent entrepreneur cross an ocean of differences to forge a love that lasts past the holidays? Come to Trappers Cove for an Over-40 Christmas beach town billionaire romance that'll steam up your windows and warm your heart!

### _Love, Legacy, and Little Green Aliens: An Over-40 Beach Town Romantic Comedy_(novel)

HEA vs. a curse, a ghost, and a plague of ETs. Inheriting his uncle's beach town souvenir shop is Xander's chance to prove he's escaped the family curse. But to transform the alien-themed embarrassment into an upscale galleria, he'll have to fight off Hannah, the gorgeous small-town journalist hell-bent on protecting Souvenir Planet. Caught in a battle of wills and sizzling desire, they discover the bizarre depths of Uncle Gus's alien obsession. Come to Trappers Cove for a steamy rivals-to-lovers rom-com full of found family, beachy fun, aliens, ghosts, and out-of-this-world mystery.

Please visit sadirastone.com and **subscribe to Sadira's bi-monthly newsletter** for bookish news, reader exclusives, and romance freebies.

# Books by Sadira Stone

## *Book Nirvana* Series

Welcome to Book Nirvana, an indie bookstore in Eugene, Oregon, where you'll find every flavor of bookish delight, a quirky staff who are as close as family, Lulu the all-wise shop cat, Coffee Dreams next door, and a dazzling collection of naughty books kept behind the red door in back. If you ask shop owner Clara nicely, she just might let you peek inside!

### *Through the Red Door*

Two good men vie to heal a widow's heart—but it only holds room for one. Unless Clara Martelli finds a lifeline, her bookstore will close its doors forever. Her best shot at saving Book Nirvana is her late husband's collection of rare, racy books, but she's not ready to open that red door. And she's not ready to open her heart again, even if the two new men in her life tempt her to try.  Come to Book Nirvana for chosen family, laughter and tears, sizzling passion, and a love triangle for the ages.

### *Runaway Love Story*

Wrong time, wrong place, perfect guy. Aspiring art gallerist Laurel is stranded in Eugene, Oregon, where she must rescue the beloved auntie who rescued her. Running into Coach Dalton ignites a sweet flirtation that quickly turns spicy. They're both enduring the heartbreak of losing a loved one to dementia. But he wants lasting love, and she's only passing through. Come to Book Nirvana for a steamy, funny, heart-wrenching tale of true love and second chances.

### *Love, Art, and Other Obstacles*

On the cusp of launching her graphic arts career, Margot is all about freedom—no fences, no limits, and no more bigoted family. Between college, work at Book Nirvana, and a high-stakes art competition, she barely has time for her part-time girlfriend, much less a flirtation with her competitor, even if his cocky, ginger-bearded hotness makes her question her "no strings" rule. Come to Book Nirvana for a red-hot love triangle that forces two young artists to redefine success, family, and freedom.

## *Bangers Tavern* Romance Series

Come to Bangers Tavern for super-steamy rom-coms featuring chosen family, diverse characters, creative cocktails, and the best tater tots in Tacoma. Four full-length novels and one novella each deliver a satisfying HEA and an unforgettable holiday bash in the neighborhood bar that feels like home. One night in Bangers, and you'll want to return again and again!

### *Christmas Rekindled*

When two Scrooges unite to save a bar in trouble, a kiss under the mistletoe sparks the steamiest Christmas miracle ever.

Bartender River hates Christmas and the sexy, snarky server who once squashed his ego. When she sashays back into Bangers Tavern, his holiday goes from blah to dismal—until a blazing hot kiss changes everything. Come to Bangers Tavern for enemies-to-lovers, fake dating, chosen family, snowed-in shenanigans, holiday cocktails, and grumpy, snarky love.

### _Opposites Ignite_

Aspiring tattoo artist Rosie is too smart to fall for her adorably straight-laced coworker at Bangers Tavern. But when they share too much New Year's Eve bubbly, Rosie wakes up in Eddie's bed! For Eddie, their New Year's surprise is a dream come true—until his grandma walks in on them. Eddie begs Rosie for a few fake dates to appease his old-fashioned family. Their lies spin out of control, and the longer he pretends, the deeper he falls.

### _Delicious Heat_

Bangers Tavern chef Diego meets a woman who makes his heart sing. Trouble is, she's pregnant with another man's child. With one belligerent ex and two overprotective families intent on breaking them up, Anna and Diego need more than red-hot passion to pull them through. His career and her baby's future are on the line. Come back to Bangers Tavern for a spicy tale of forbidden love that will warm your heart...and other parts...and make you hungry for empanadas!

### _Sweet Slow Sizzle_

Bangers Tavern's hunky bouncer Jojo has been crushing on server Lana for years, but her sole focus is keeping her orphaned brothers together in the only home they've ever known. When their teen shenanigans land them in trouble, Jojo may be the only person who can save them. This slow burn, sizzling hot friends-to-lovers workplace romance celebrates the glorious chaos of 21st century family—the ones we're born into, and the ones we gather to our hearts.

### *Cupid's Silver Spark: A Bangers Tavern Novella*

At Bangers Tavern's Anti-Valentine's bash, vintage shop owner Carla collides with a swoonworthy silver fox. Could a no-strings fling be the remedy for her tattered heart? He seems perfect for the job: suave, attentive, and oh so tempting. Trouble is, his real estate firm has the hots for her building. To keep her business, Carla must dare to trust the enemy. Will her silver fox prove a predator, or will Cupid's arrow strike true?

Please visit sadirastone.com and **subscribe to Sadira's bi-monthly newsletter** for bookish news, reader exclusives,and romance freebies.

# About the author

Award-winning contemporary romance author Sadira Stone spins steamy, smoochy tales set in the U.S. Pacific Northwest. Her stories highlight found family, friendship, and the sizzling chemistry that pulls unlikely partners together. When she emerges from her writing cave in Las Vegas, Nevada (which she seldom does), she can be found shaking her hips in dance class, blowing bubbles with her granddaughter, playing her guitar (not very well, but improving!), exploring the Western U.S. with her charming husband, cooking up a storm, and gobbling all the romance books. For a guaranteed HEA (and no cliffhangers!) visit Sadira at sadirastone.com.

**Visit Sadira on all the socials!**
**https://linktr.ee/SadiraStone**

www.ingramcontent.com/pod-product-compliance
Lightning Source LLC
Chambersburg PA
CBHW031055310726
48969CB00007B/2286